READ ME IN A PEDALO
Issue nº 11 — Summer 2018

G000255287

PART 1

On the cover, singer OLLY ALEXANDER photograp
Daniel Riera with styling by Stuart Williamson

PART 2

The Book of the Season is THE BLACK TULIP by Alexandre
Dumas, originally written in French and published in 1850 as LA
TULIPE NOIRE

A quintessential scene
of seaside reading,
captured here by
MARTIN PARR.

CONTINUE READING

Nobody gets rich by selling bookmarks. Train tickets, card receipts, coupons for distant pizzerias: the transient paper of everyday life is determined to undercut anyone who might try.

It hasn't always been this way. There was a time when the bookmark was a more important mode of self-expression, and so the reader would cherish those that weren't moonlighting. A bookmark might be made from precious metal, skilfully fabricated by a jeweller of note: Tiffany & Co and House of Fabergé each produced *haute* bookmarks. A wafer of solid silver, glimpsable in a reader's Dumas, might be shaped like a woman's hand, a rabbit, a skull or an ornate trowel; the bookmark worth far more than the book. And why not, for something that will last a century? A 100-year-old enamel-and-gold marker from St Petersburg sold at auction in 2003 for £3,346 and it's hard to imagine it went straight into that year's big page-turner *The Da Vinci Code*.

The bookmark was to bookishness what the neck-scarf is to fashion. Today it is more like the sock. But still, even our socks end up communicating something about us.

New York-based rare-book dealer Michael Popek runs a website, Forgotten Bookmarks, on which he shares the flat things he finds between the pages of his acquisitions. Each meeting of book and placeholder grasps at a story. In a crime novel: a blurry photograph of a cyclist struggling through the snow. In a hardback about battlefields: a print-on-demand bookmark commemorating a wedding.

Shoelaces, city maps, floral colour charts: if our bookmark can entertain those sitting opposite us on the train or on a neighbouring towel on the beach, it should. Low-value banknotes are a pleasing parody of conspicuous consumption (as Steven Spielberg said, 'Why pay a dollar for a bookmark? Why not use the dollar as a bookmark?'). Playing cards grant the reader an enigmatic aura (tarot is too much). Purpose-made bookmarks are great, if chosen with care. Just don't be revolting like the person in Worthing who once returned a library book containing a raw rasher of bacon.

THE HAPPY READER
Bookish Magazine
Issue nº 11 — Summer 2018

The Happy Reader is
a collaboration between
Penguin Books and
Fantastic Man

EDITOR-IN-CHIEF
Seb Emina

EDITORIAL DIRECTORS
Jop van Bennekom
Gert Jonkers

MANAGING EDITOR
Maria Bedford

DESIGN
Tom Etherington

DESIGN CONCEPT
Jop van Bennekom
Helios Capdevila

PICTURE RESEARCH
Samantha Johnson

PRODUCTION
Alice Burkle

PUBLISHER
Helen Conford

MARKETING DIRECTOR
Nicola Hill

BRAND DIRECTOR
Sam Voulters

MANAGING DIRECTOR
Stefan McGrath

CONTRIBUTORS
Richard Benson, Thomas Bird,
Charlie Connelly, Jean Hannah
Edelstein, Paul Flynn, Neal
Fox, Eliot Haworth, Jane C. Hu,
Rebecca May Johnson, Jordan
Kelly, Deborah Levy, Jamie
MacRae, Aaron Peck, Daniel
Riera, Stuart Williamson.

THANK YOU
Magnus Åkesson, Naomi
Alderman, Alice Cavanagh,
Linda Fallon, Camille Ferté,
Maggie Koerth-Baker,
Rebecca Lee, Ruth Pietroni,
Caroline Pretty, Antonia
Webb, Julie Woon.

Penguin Books
80 Strand
London WC2R 0RL

info@thehappyreader.com
www.thehappyreader.com

SNIPPETS

Summer's news and gossip from the farthest-flung reaches of literary life.

IMPERIAL — Technology giant Apple has commissioned a TV series based on Isaac Asimov's *Foundation* books. The cult sci-fi novels depict an attempt to avert the collapse of a giant galactic empire.

PLAID — London-based writer A.N. Devers has launched a business dedicated to selling rare books (and associated paraphernalia) by women. The company, which goes by the name The Second Shelf, has acquired sought-after signed books by authors such as Joan Didion, Toni Morrison and Muriel Spark, plus artefacts including a tartan plaid skirt that belonged to the poet Sylvia Plath.

HOMEWORK — Ahead of Prince Harry's wedding to Meghan Markle, the bride's father, Thomas Markle Sr, was spotted in a branch of Starbucks near his home in Mexico, dutifully browsing a hardback entitled *Images of Britain: A Pictorial Journey Through History*.

THINKER — Rapper and entrepreneur Kanye West is writing a philosophy book entitled *Break the Simulation*. Or perhaps it's safer to say philosophy-*ish*: 'Let's say it's just a concept,' he hedged in an interview, 'because sometimes philosophy sounds too heavy-handed.'

MEMENTO — Georgia Grainger, a librarian in Dundee, Scotland, was baffled when a customer asked, 'Why does page 7 in all the books I take out have the 7 underlined in pen?' Having checked and found this to be true, Grainger realised the vandalised books were all the same kind, specifically that which elderly ladies tend to enjoy: romances set in wartime Britain, that type of thing. Which is how the mystery was solved: the underlining is an example of the secret marks elderly clientele make inside library books to ensure they don't read the same one twice.

VERSE — The best year on record for sales of poetry in the UK was... 2017. Not only were over a million poetry books sold, sending over £11 million through poetry-peddling cash registers, but more people than ever are writing the stuff: the most recent survey on this subject revealed that fully 3 per cent of the adult population of England, or 1.4 million people, wrote some poetry between 2015 and 2016.

ARTY — Actor Keanu Reeves was seen in Paris for the European launch of X Artists' Books, an LA-based publishing company he founded with artist Alexandra Grant and designer Jessica Fleischmann. Initial releases include *High Winds*, a really quite beautiful art book described as a 'picture book for adults'.

CHART — New York Public Library revealed its most borrowed title in 2017, across all branches throughout New York City, to have been Ta-Nehisi Coates' meditation on race, *Between the World and Me*.

PISS OFF — Scientists ask that fans of Henry David Thoreau stop peeing in his famous pond. Every year, around half a million tourists visit Walden Pond in Massachusetts, USA, the setting for Thoreau's 1854 wilderness memoir *Walden; or, Life in the Woods*. Now, a study has revealed that over half the phosphorus in the lake during summer may be 'attributable to urine released by swimmers'.

NOVEL — The one-time residence of *Don Quixote* author Miguel de Cervantes is available as a holiday rental. Located in Barcelona's Gothic Quarter, the sizeable duplex sleeps five.

OLLY ALEXANDER

In conversation with
PAUL FLYNN

Portraits by
DANIEL RIERA

Three hundred million: that's how many times the Years & Years song 'King' has been streamed online by a single provider. Just one song. Yet despite these absurd metrics, the British band's singer and this season's *Happy Reader* interviewee has remained a really nice guy. Perhaps that's the legacy of a youth spent enjoying (among other things) a spree of very good books. This unique interview — also covering sexuality, stardom and the travails of moving to London from a small town on the Welsh border — reveals much about the many paradoxes of the massive pop star named OLLY ALEXANDER.

LONDON

By sheer coincidence, the last occasion I met Olly Alexander before this interview was to talk about books. I'd recorded the pilot for a podcast about A Gay Book That Changed My Life and Olly was the first intrepid subject, talking eloquently about the mesmerising story-telling of James Baldwin's *Giovanni's Room*. Olly's always a pleasure but was particularly engaging on the book and its importance. It struck me more than once during the conversation that it's often those who leave school early and educate themselves who have the clearest, sharpest love of literature. Books remain pure, felt experiences, their spines unsaturated by the stuffy rigours of academia.

I first met Olly at the start of his career as the frontman of Years & Years, though I'd noticed him around a lot before that. It's always funny when somebody from your neighbourhood becomes famous. He hung around some of the gay pubs and clubs I'd frequent and it didn't take long to work out I recognised him from some of the screen roles which predated his pop life.

Olly has stuffed a lot of living into his twenty-seven years. For a brief moment before Years & Years began their pop ride, it looked as if he might become a famous actor. He was directed by Gaspar Noé in the brilliantly dystopian drama *Enter the Void*, which he filmed at seventeen over two bracing months in Tokyo. He starred in Belle and Sebastian front-man Stuart Murdoch's deeply whimsical feature film, *God Help the Girl*, as a love-struck musician roaming Glasgow's West End. He fleetingly had a role in *Skins*, the Channel 4 drama which took a scalpel to the teenage lives and loves of generation MySpace (in both the digital and literal senses of the expression).

I'd always wondered whether being around these idiosyncratic storytellers at such a young age had affected his own artistry. Years & Years pulls off a deft balancing act. They are an accessible, mass-market pop act who have something interesting to say for themselves. They win Brit Awards and have sold three million copies of their album *Communion* around the world. Olly has managed to weave into this commercial largesse a gentle generational figurehead position, particularly with regard to the hot-button subjects of LGBTQI equality and mental health. He is the most useful vanguard pop star to mirror the gay culture's diametric shift from a predominant interest in our exterior lives to that of our interior patterns; like a perkier, junior John Grant to a disco beat. Young fans see him as a friend as much as a star.

To my delight, a gay book that changed my life, Andrew Holleran's *Dancer from the Dance* — the book often playfully dubbed 'The Gay Gatsby' — is referenced in the seamlessly effective first Years & Years song, 'Sanctify', to be taken from their impending second album, *Palo Santo*. Our first interview takes place one spring afternoon at a bakery near London Fields, ten minutes equidistant from our flats. We talk until closing time, at which point we have to be politely chucked out.

1. POEM BY YEATS

'O body swayed to music,
O brightening glance, /
How can we know the
dancer from the dance?'
W B Yeats, 1933

PAUL: There's a reference to the amazing *Dancer from the Dance* in 'Sanctify'. Is that the first literary reference you've dropped into a pop hit?

OLLY: I think so. I can't think of anything else.

P: Why that one?

O: Well, I'd just read the book. It was given to me by an ex-boyfriend. I hadn't heard of it before. I just saw the cover and the little blurb and thought, 'I'm down to read this.' The main character goes from this straight lawyer to being immersed in pre-Aids gay New York, which sounds so intoxicating and alive and vibrant. Fire Island is going on. It reads like this merry-go-round of pleasure and pain, an amazing time to be alive. When I started to write the new record I was thinking, 'What is my voice?' I want to, at least in my own small way, add to that long list of queer artists that speak of their own experience.

P: Did reading the book correlate directly to writing the song?

O: I think so. I'd been thinking a lot about straight men, or men who identify as straight but want to explore their sexuality but don't feel like they're able to. Reading *Dancer from the Dance* was the catalyst that made me think, 'Yes, I'm going to do this.' I just thought of that title line, I think it's from a poem by Yeats? 'How can we know the dancer from the dance?' It touches on so many things that I feel are so important about the experience of discovering your sexuality, which is so tied to me with going dancing, being in clubs with bodies surrounding you, of losing yourself in the music; of how much that is its own church. I've always fed those themes into the music.

P: Do you know much about Andrew Holleran?

O: No.

P: Are you interested to?

O: Oh yes.

Olly's trainers are by Kiko
Kostadinov × ASICS, his
socks are by Falke, his
jumpsuit is by Dickies, and
his book is by Alexandre
Dumas. Yes, he's reading
The Black Tulip.

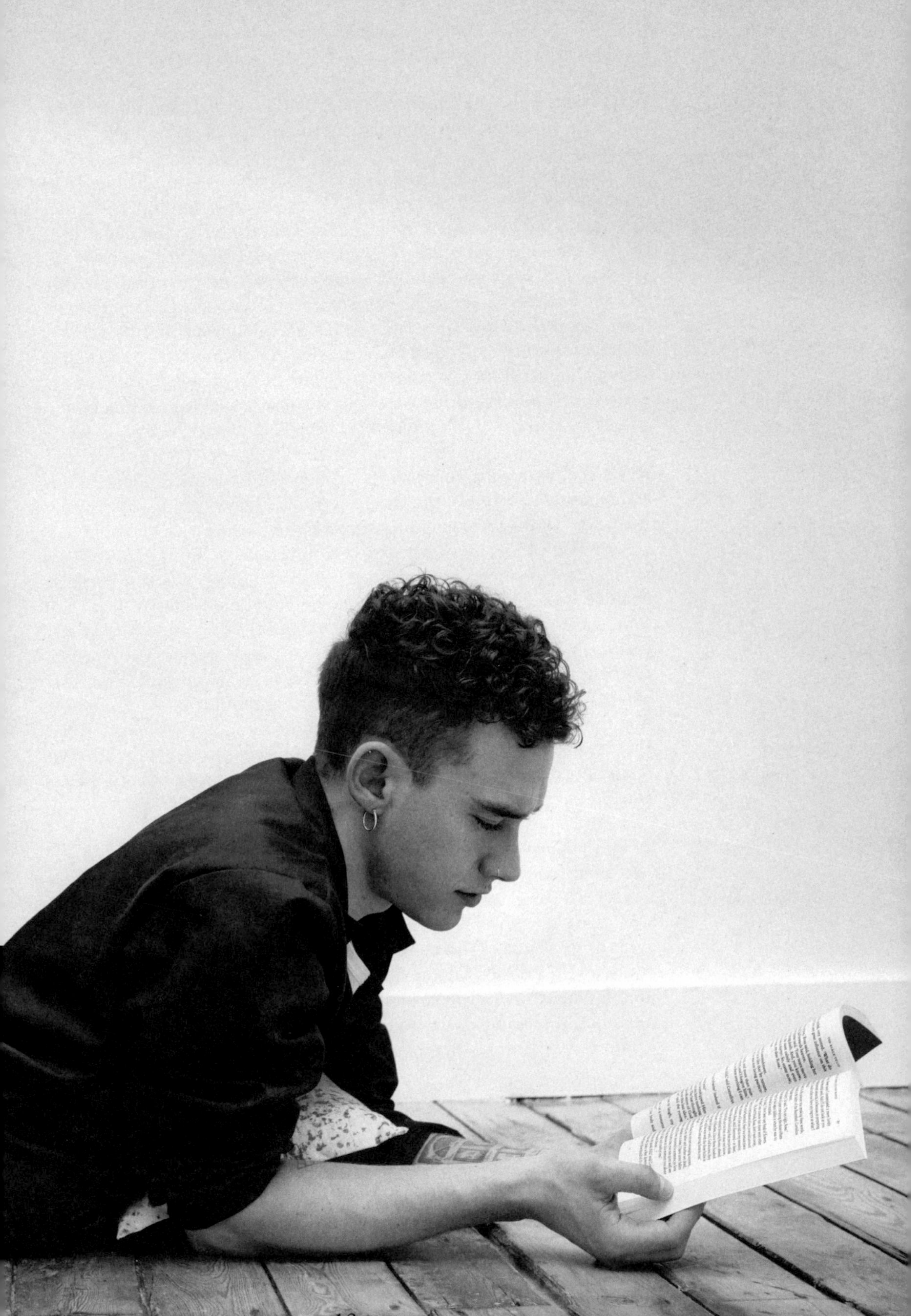

P: The last book he wrote as far as I know was called *Grief*.

O: Oh God. I mean, *Dancer from the Dance* is pretty bleak.

P: He really nails the beautiful sadness of the discotheque in it. How much can someone your age relate to the golden New York age of the emergence of disco?

O: I didn't feel like I knew much about any of it until I met [legendary New York nightlife royalty] Larry Tee, just through going out in London. I'd hang out with him quite a lot in the back room at East Bloc. It became part of my weekend routine. Larry had so many insane stories. They opened up a completely different world to me. We all have a tendency to romanticise the years that have gone before us, but around the same time I watched *Paris is Burning* and then *Party Monster* and they started to open the door into what New York nightlife was. I'm still discovering it now. Part of me wishes I could've experienced it and the other part feels it's just laced with so much pain and sadness that I don't know if I'd want to go back there.

P: Of the two central characters, Malone, the beautiful nightlife ingénue, and Sutherland, the waspish grande dame casting his eye over it all, who do you feel you'd most like to be friends with?

O: Well, I feel like I have known quite a lot of Sutherlands. What I thought was so good about *Dancer from the Dance* was that because Malone is so beautiful and everyone he encounters falls in love with him, the book could go into the toxic side of the pursuit of beauty and youth. Each season there's a hot new boy. The last one is discarded. It's brutal. It's savage. But that thing rings true to me still. I felt that when I was going out all the time. Who is the hot boy? Who is the boy that will always bring the looks? Who's the boy who always has the drugs? Who is the one with the best music taste? There is this status-obsessed animal kingdom in any community or social circle. It's total anthropology.

P: Did you have a fleeting moment of being the hot new boy, and was that in any way a dress rehearsal for fame?

O: In some ways, yes. That's why it's so intoxicating. It's why I was going out every weekend. You start to get to know people and it was the one time of the week where I could be anybody. I'll wear this tonight. I'll be this person. In the middle of the dancefloor there is that moment where you're lost in it all and you feel invincible. Sometimes I did feel powerful but then in the space of the same night you could feel crushingly depressed and empty, too.

P: We should probably point out here that your entrance into the nightlife was as a teenager, in London, coming from a small town on the Welsh borders.

O: Yes.

P: You plunged yourself right in the deep end.

O: Yes.

P: Had you even had the practice run of a parochial gay bar before you entered London nightlife?

O: Oh no, never. I moved to London when I was eighteen and at the time I wasn't even calling myself gay. I'm trying to think of the first gay bar I ever went to.

P: I'm assuming it wasn't a beautiful metropolitan experience surrounded by the cream of intellectual and physical excellence that Andrew Holleran writes about?

O: Sadly not. It was probably the Joiners Arms. Which had its own charm, of course. Oh no, I remember what it was. When I was fifteen I did a National Youth Theatre course. We were with a group of maybe thirty other people, staying in university halls of residence. I'd never been away from Coleford, really. I was really quite overwhelmed by everything. One night we said, 'Shall we go to Soho?' Because we were all underage we decided that the only way we could get in anywhere was to flirt with the bouncers at a gay bar. That made sense, right? And it worked. We went to Ku Bar and I remember being completely terrified. Everyone was looking at each other, sizing each other up. I was fifteen, maybe sixteen, which is pretty young to feel the gaze of other men. I remember it being quite traumatising. That first night, I remember a guy touching me completely inappropriately and being kind of excited, kind of turned on and kind of repulsed by it. I didn't go back to another gay club for another three years. That one would be the Joiners.

P: It's funny that first threshold crossed, moving from a world where gay is almost invisible to one where it's so disarmingly visible, from the consciousness of being a minority to suddenly being in the majority. Like, what is this new world? What are the new codes I have to learn? Are these now 'my people'? If so, who are they?

O: It's a minefield. Suddenly you're in strange new territory.

P: What about the other side of that, the bravery it takes to accept who you are at fifteen, making that active decision to stick your head in the lion's mouth?

O: There is something to be said about a baptism of fire. Maybe it takes you to a place that otherwise you might not have got to tread. You do learn from that experience. It forges something strong inside of you.

P: What did you move to London for?

O: Just to get out, as quickly as possible. I got an acting agent when I was seventeen and had two jobs back-to-back really quickly. My agent said if you want to keep acting then move to London. I'd made enough money to put a deposit down on a flat, to rent for a bit. My mum drove me to this flat. She only told me recently that she cried when she dropped me off. The room had no windows and a mattress on the floor. It was tiny. I think she was like, 'My god, I'm leaving my son in a windowless cupboard in Bethnal Green. What have I done?'

P: Do you remember that first London address?

O: 12b Granby Street. Just off Brick Lane. Such a shithole. I knew the girl I was living with, she was a friend of a friend. Other than that, I didn't know anybody in London. It's quite a hard city if you don't know anybody.

P: London is a generally horrible place for teenagers to live in because it's so status and money obsessed.

O: I was lucky I'd had this cash injection from acting jobs. I was making way more money than all my friends who were doing minimum-wage jobs. But that went so quickly and then I was working fifty hours a week in a bar.

P: What were those jobs?

O: I had quite a few. I worked at Polpo, then at another restaurant they had called Spuntino.

P: Oh, I lived in that place when it first opened, you must've served me.

O: Probably. It was a really good restaurant. I worked on a hot-dog van. I'd have acting jobs in between, so I'd make a bit of money, be OK for six months, then have to live off pasta for the next month.

P: Was there ever a point you thought you'd have to go home?

O: Yes. I was ten grand in debt, a combination of overdraft and people who'd lent me money. I could never afford to pay my tax bill, because nobody ever teaches you how the fuck you're supposed to do that. I didn't have anywhere to live, so I was living with my friend whose dad had a place in an unfinished building. There was no shower or bathroom. We'd eat cup-a-soups and listen to the radio for

2. GRANBY STREET

An online review of a Granby St holiday apartment describes the road thus: 'One side of the neigbourhood (Shoreditch and Brick Lane) was very nice, but the other (Bethnal Green) rather shady. At night there were always some cars randomly parked on the street with someone waiting inside.'

entertainment, like we were in the war or something. [laughing] That was the only point I thought, 'Right, I don't live anywhere.'

P: Were all your friends made through nightlife?
O: Yes, pretty much.

P: Were there musical aspirations at that time?
O: I'd moved primarily just to get away from my small-town life. I thought maybe I'd become this big actor. I was always in bands and had always written music, and then when I moved to London I brought my little keyboard with me, but I didn't have any outlet for it. I really started to miss it. Then when I was nineteen, I met Mikey [Goldsworthy] and he said he wanted to start a band, did I want to play with them? That was the start of Years & Years.

P: You've been ten years in the city?
O: This year is my tenth.

P: What are the songs that most strongly remind you of just having moved here?
O: From the first MGMT album, 'Time to Pretend' and 'Kids'. There was a Santigold song ['L.E.S. Artistes'], the one where she's on a horse in the video. I would make CDs for boys that I liked and put those songs on. Eighteen seems so young now. I know I'm only twenty-seven but those ten years are a long time.

P: They're marked by such a radically changed circumstance for you, from only having a radio to listen to, to being on it all the time.
O: Yes, I suppose. I was lying in bed thinking about this interview last night and having this real moment of, fuck, my life is actually insane. What's happened to me? I've moved into a new flat and it's big and I have no furniture. I'm buying furniture for the first time. I am aware that I'm in quite an extraordinary position here, too. Most of my friends are struggling to pay their rent. I was there, only four years ago. It's just a strange thing.

P: How important have books been for you in teaching yourself about LGBT history?
O: I wouldn't know otherwise where to start. We're not taught it in schools. You have to go out to find who our queer ancestors and family are. There's a lot of conflicting information. It's not super easy for people to tap into. For me, reading James Baldwin's *Giovanni's Room* — I mean, amazing — another book an old boyfriend gave me, or even just discovering gay characters in books that at the time I

3. MIKEY

Bassist Mikey Goldsworthy asked Olly to join the band after overhearing him singing in the shower the morning after a house party. Recalling this in an interview Olly said the song 'was probably "Killing Me Softly" because that's my shower song.'

didn't realise would have them in. I can't think of an example here, of course.

P: The recent one I particularly loved is that amazing gay character Jennifer Egan slots into *A Visit from the Goon Squad*, towards the end. Another sad, beautiful boy looking around Manhattan nightlife for answers, but this time during the early '90s and Grunge.

    O: True. Oh my God. That chapter is actually amazing. I just read *Manhattan Beach*, actually.

P: It's such a different beast to *Goon Squad* I feel like it's got a little lost, but I loved it just as much. Did you like it?

    O: Yes, I did.

P: I love the gangster character.

    O: The one she fucks in the barn? That's a really hot scene. I loved the protagonist. I also read *Look at Me*, her book about the model. That really affected me. Like, how is she nailing this hunger for fame so well? I know what that feels like because I've had it. She has this metaphor for fame, which is a bright mirrored room with all these famous faces in it at the top of this amazing building, where they're all being powerful and amazing and she just wants to be there among them all. Obviously at the end of the novel she realises it's completely empty and all those people are just shells and she wants an interior life, so she moves away from it. I found that whole book really smart and true. How does she know that stuff?

P: How many books do you start to those you finish?

    O: Oh, I always finish a book. I just feel like if I've committed I have to finish it. To be honest, it's not worth pushing through if you're not enjoying it and I don't know why I do it. Self-flagellation? I started reading *The Line of Beauty*. I'm only 100 pages in. I think I like it. I don't know yet.

P: I just read *The Sparsholt Affair*, and the first part of it with all those fussy Oxford academics made me want to firebomb the place.

    O: Yes, I get that a lot of writers have been through that experience and want to write about it because it's so close to them. But if you haven't? I kind of got that with Donna Tartt's *The Secret History*. That's a world I know nothing about, but she takes you into it. It's all so accessible and available to you.

P: It makes Ivy League universities feel like *The Breakfast Club*.

    O: I liked *The Goldfinch* too.

OLLY ALEXANDER

Olly loves reading and sees no harm in maltreating books to put them in shape.

Cover for the single 'Time to Pretend' (2007) by American rock band MGMT (p.17). The song is partly inspired by, in the sense it has exactly the same tempo as, ABBA's 'Dancing Queen' (1976).

Badge representing love for (or at least knowledge of) Glaswegian party night Optimo (Espacio) (p.22). Non-Glaswegians: tune into their monthly online radio show on NTS.

Credit still from *Enter the Void* (2009) by Argentinian director Gaspar Noé (p.23). Concept: the afterlife but experienced by a French drug dealer living in Tokyo.

Red canvas jacket worn by River Phoenix in *My Own Private Idaho* (1992) (p.33). Sold at auction in 2012 for $3,125 (£2,181).

Flag of Gloucestershire, where Olly grew up. The Severn Cross has been the county's official flag for just eight years, having won a competition held by the so-titled High Sheriff of Gloucestershire.

George Michael (p.26), who died in 2016. Michael found fame as a member of the pop duo Wham!, with whom he sold 30 million records, before going on to sell a further 80 million as a solo artist.

Years & Years are Mikey Goldsworthy, Olly Alexander and Emre Türkmen.

A box containing sachets of 'pea and ham flavour' cup-a-soup (p.16), the derided instant food product that is, and seemingly has always been, available from every grocery shop in the world.

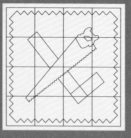

Neil Tennant and Chris Lowe, aka Pet Shop Boys (p.28). Even taking into account Eurythmics, Erasure, Shakespears Sister and Chas & Dave, Pet Shop Boys are the most successful duo in the history of British music with over 100 million records sold.

Joining-related insignia from the wall of East London LGBT pub the Joiners Arms (p.15). The Joiners, as it's known, closed in 2015, though a campaign is under way to bring it back.

James Baldwin (pp.17, 26), American literary legend and civil rights advocate.

DJ, music producer and promoter Larry Tee (p.14), who helped launch the careers of RuPaul and Peaches, and coined the term 'electroclash'.

Hilton Als (p.26), one of America's most stylish prose writers. His next book will apparently explore James Baldwin, black masculinity and the literary world.

Taking its name from the colloquialism for either cigarette rolling papers or condoms, British television drama *Skins* (p.21) documented the hedonism, hijinks and heartbreak of fictional Bristolian teenagers in their final two years of sixth form college.

Olly mulls with co-stars Emily Browning (Eve) and Hannah Murray (Cassie) in *God Help the Girl* (2014) (p.22), about friends starting a band in Glasgow. Olly's character, James, is a lifeguard as well as a budding songwriter.

A still from the documentary film *Paris is Burning* (1990) (p.14), chronicling the catwalk competitions and vogue dancing battles of New York City's ball culture.

P: Loved. I always think that people who don't like *The Goldfinch* are the readers who've never been the fourteen-year-old that would steal the painting.

O: Interesting. My God, that's blown my mind. [thinks for a second] I would've stolen it.

P: Of course you would have done. You have that hand-in-the-fire approach to life.

O: Yes. That's true. It's something that has been said to me before that I hadn't considered. But now, when I look back on things I did, I can't quite believe that I did them. I don't ever feel super confident.

P: Have you talked to anyone about that?

O: Oh yeah, I've spent a lot of money on working that out. I've seen various counsellors and therapists since I was a teenager. I've had the same therapist since the year before we got signed to the record label. I honestly think it's life-saving in a way.

P: Does talking to a therapist enable your storytelling capacity?

O: Yes, I think so. I want to be as open as possible. I want to go to places that mean something to me, that touch the pain inside myself and make it a little bit easier to cope with.

P: I wanted to ask about a few of the storytellers that you've been around professionally. The first is Brian Elsley, the man behind *Skins*.

O: God, there's a blast from the past. I met Brian first when I was sixteen. I went to an open casting for the show. I nearly got a part and didn't. I was only in a couple of episodes towards the end of it and it was a totally different thing by then. All the things that seemed so new about it when it started weren't new any more. But it was such a touchstone at the start, everyone was talking about it. It was the first portrayal of British youth that tried to talk in their language. You hadn't seen anything like that on TV before, not for my generation at least. I have a very funny relationship with that show because it was my first experience of a professional acting environment. Then, at any given time, I would work with or knew almost every cast member. April [Pearson], Larissa [Wilson], Hannah [Murray], Nick [Hoult], Dev [Patel], I knew them all. I had a couple of auditions with Mitch [Hewer], who played Maxxie, and I remember being so in love with him when the show came out.

4. SKINS °

Olly appeared in 'Skins Redux', the TV show's 7th (and final) season, in which he played Jakob, an obsessive photographer.

P: My two favourite success stories from that programme, the ones that really get me, are Daniel Kaluuya and Jack O'Connell. Did you ever work with them?

O: Yes, me and Jack very nearly did a movie together. It fell through, but we were rehearsing together for a week. It was called *U Want Me 2 Kill Him?* and it did get made in the end but not with us. The rehearsals were really weird. Bryan Singer was producing it. The whole storyline was me being a bit in love with Jack's character, and I could just see how it would've played out and happened for real.

P: Had you slightly fallen in love with him during that week?

O: I think so. He's just got so much charisma he does bowl you over. He's completely firing on all cylinders all the time.

P: There's nothing to him. He's a scrap of a man, but there are visible sparks flying off him.

O: Yes, oh absolutely.

P: The next storyteller I wanted to ask about was Stuart Murdoch.

O: I love him. He's a really fascinating guy. As an actor you never really get jobs that you want to do. You take what's offered. Then a Belle and Sebastian movie comes along. I wrote my own song for the audition. Stuart said, 'That was exactly what the character would've done so I instantly gave you the part.' Such a dream job. Every day you're hanging out with other musicians, it's Glasgow, and I got to sing and play an actual good role. It was super indie, low budget.

P: If you think about Stuart from Belle and Sebastian making a film, that film is pretty much exactly what you'd imagine.

O: Stuart's a really unique voice in British music. He's quite a bizarre, surrealist figure. He's always blowing his nose. There's always a hanky. When we started filming I thought maybe Stuart was gay. There's a femininity to him and he likes to play around with that a bit. Then I met his wife. The character was based on Stuart and there was always this slight tension that I never told him I was gay. I felt like I had to keep a pretence that I might be straight because I was meant to be in love with Hannah [Murray]'s character. I was twenty-two. It was quite stressful with this tiny cast who knew that I was gay but I was sort of trying to hide it at the same time. Then one night I went to the Optimo night at Sub Club, met this guy and ended up going out with him for the rest of the movie. I'd shoot all day and then go back to his flat all night.

P: What was his name?

O: Andrew. He was really sweet, actually.

P: The third storyteller was Gaspar Noé.

5. BELLE AND SEBASTIAN

The name of Scottish indie band Belle and Sebastian is a literary reference by two degrees. The inspiration was a French children's TV series, which was in turn an adaptation of the novel *Belle et Sébastien* by Cécile Aubry, about a six-year old boy living in the Alps called Sébastien, and his dog Belle.

O: It's funny you're asking about these guys. I can see why you'd bring those men up, but the thing is, when I was an actor, for most of my career I was just terrified about what people would say about me being gay. You could not be gay as an actor. I did not know any out gay actors. I knew Ben Whishaw. I'd met him when I was seventeen and acted with him, but even Ben wasn't really out then. People sort of knew, but he hadn't said it in an interview yet. He's seven or eight years older than me. I massively looked up to him. I still would say we're quite close. He's a wonderful, magical creature.

P: You played a gay character in *Enter the Void* though?

O: I met Gaspar when I was seventeen and all these crazy things were happening. Living in Tokyo for two months, filming with Gaspar, playing this character who was gay and in love with his straight best friend. I mean, art imitating life again here. I'd been in love with my friend at school and that had turned out horribly. I got this movie playing a gay guy when I was in the closet to myself, really. Then I was falling in love with the actor on-set in the main role and we'd spend every minute of every day together, and Gaspar, I think, knew that this was going on. I was going through a lot of inner turmoil about my own sexuality and that was played out in this weird way for a role on-screen in Tokyo.

P: Do you like the film?

O: I mean, I watched it once and it was quite hard to watch. I can't believe I was a part of it.

P: Are you in some ways glad that period of your life is documented, however obliquely?

O: Hmm, I don't know. I think so? It's good that it was Gaspar. It's not like you can see me struggling into my sexuality on an episode of *Holby City*.

6. HOLBY CITY

The television show *Holby City* proves there's no corner of culture left untouched by the ravages of fan fiction. Users of the site fanfiction.net have written over 1,800 short stories set in the BBC hospital drama's universe.

Olly turns 28 on 15 July 2018. Styling: Stuart Williamson. Photographic assistance: Matt Lain. Styling assistance: Jamie MacRae. Grooming: Michael Harding.

RE-READING & RE-MEETING

We meet for a second time, two weeks later, in a coffee shop just off Kingsland Road, east London. Easter weekend is incoming. Olly has by this point begun rehearsals for the live realisation of *Palo Santo*.

Somewhat shamefully, before Olly chose it as the gay book that changed his life, I'd never read *Giovanni's Room*. Since he had introduced me to such a masterpiece, I set him a little homework between interviews and handed over a copy of Hilton Als' *White Girls* to read in the interim, the *New Yorker* theatre critic's collection of mightily impressive, sprawling essays on culture, race and sexuality. The connecting tissue is that Als refers often to Baldwin throughout his work, and not always in a complimentary way. His supposition is that Baldwin was ultimately ruined by his desire to be, above all else, a 'famous writer'. It felt like this might be a good opening to talk about Olly's didactic relationship to his fame and his forebears.

I left the first conversation determined to do a bit of homework of my own by re-reading *Dancer from the Dance*. I first read it as a nineteen-year-old in Manchester, while working in a record shop and living in the city's pivotal nightclubs of the late '80s. Twenty-eight years later it read, if anything, even more seismic and epochal than it did as a teenager, at an age when I precociously understood some but far from all of the book's themes. The second time around, it felt almost biblical. I couldn't stop thinking about it, and about the passing of time from being a very young man, a Malone, to being one who thinks he's seen it all, a Sutherland.

I've found this with Olly on the many times we've met professionally. He has a charismatic superpower which always gives you the impression of wanting to learn something from you while doing most of the teaching himself. I think, as we stand in 2018, he's just about Britain's best pop star, for numerous reasons, far from all of them related to pop music.

PAUL: Are there limitations to being a pop musician that you don't get in other jobs?

OLLY: Limitations in what way?

P: Do you ever feel like you have to be a less complicated, even potentially less interesting version of yourself to operate in the mass market?

O: Oh yes, all the time. I feel like there's pressure from all sorts of angles to make yourself less interesting than you really are. At the end of the day, if you are signed to a major record label then your main objective is to make your label a lot of money. We've had a great time at the label. They've been supportive. But, to an extent, everyone's scared of risk, which is such a shame. Also, I feel, completely counterintuitively, because the great pop acts have all broken the mould and done something that proves that's what people want. But you get to a stage where it's not just me and the band making something. It's me and the band making something for a label that suddenly involves hundreds of other people. It's quite hard to stem all of those voices all of the time. Not always. I mean, the label has supported us.

P: Do you think you put limitations on yourself to send yourself out to market?

O: I don't know. I want what I do to be true to Years & Years, but I want people to like it, so that it functions as a pop band. There's always that tension between wanting to be completely indulgent and it reaching our audience.

P: The reason I asked you to read the Hilton Als book was because I love the way he audaciously undercuts James Baldwin in it. Does the idea of killing your idols appeal to you?

O: I feel like there's definitely a drive within me that in part was created by a desire to do it better than whoever I'd seen do it before.

P: Was that about pop music or specifically gay pop music?

O: I wasn't really aware of any gay pop music, apart from George Michael, and that felt like he had come before my time and his story was really one that I didn't connect to. I connected in other ways — of course his songwriting is absolutely amazing. But he was so assertive in his sexuality. He was sexy.

P: During his commercial primacy he was heterosexy, or an imitation of heterosexy that satisfied all the basic mass-market impulses.

O: I was aware of that being part of his narrative too, that he was in the closet for a really long time, then something kind of shady happened and I wasn't even sure what it was. Did he fuck a guy in public? Then he crashed his car. All that stuff. My mum loved him. The songs are so good. Most of my favourite singers were female, then I also really idolised Stevie Wonder and Jeff Buckley, but it felt like coming up against a barrier or a wall when they talked about women. I really wanted a musician that I could identify with. There was a part of me that felt like I've got something to say. I felt like I'd

---

7. JEFF BUCKLEY

Cult singer-songwriter in the 90s, whose haunting music took on an even more tragic tone after he drowned during a midnight swim, aged just 30. Today Buckley's version of 'Hallelujah' is famous around the world: the song had a 15-year genesis through its writer Leonard Cohen and covers including one by John Cale before Buckley recorded the definitive, delicately mournful, interpretation.

got something to prove and like I could do it. The counter of that is that you don't think you're good enough and nobody is going to give you a shot. But then both can exist at the same time. It's funny.

P: I wonder whether the negative voice, of not knowing whether you're going to be given a chance to be heard, is more of a driving force than the wanting to prove you should be?

O: Oh, totally. My dad wanted to be a musician and that played into it. I remember always being bullied at school and just thinking, 'One day I'm going to be on top of the world.' Imagining that it would make me feel so powerful and that I'd slay all these demons. In a weird way, I don't think that leaves you. This little seed got planted that if I could be this successful, this powerful, this glamorous, this hot, this attractive, then I could right all these wrongs. And I know now that isn't the case. But there's still a part of me that believes it. It's just bizarre.

P: It's the oldest driver of fame in the book and it manifests itself in a lot of gay men. Have you read *The Velvet Rage*?

O: Yes. Of course.

P: In retrospect, I feel like Alan Downs doesn't identify anything in that therapy book that wasn't said in *Dancer from the Dance* forty years earlier, in a so much more beautiful way and without all the soft-speak Californian psychobabble.

O: *The Velvet Rage* was helpful to me. It was given to me by an ex-boyfriend. Every fucking book that I keep talking about seems to have been. But I do think there's something in that, that we have to as gay men, just to divert slightly, we have to go on our own discovery and build our own connections between each other because we are not handed those things. I remember with *The Velvet Rage* I couldn't quite believe that somebody had written about things that I had felt. But after I'd finished it I wasn't quite sure I agreed with it or that it resonated with my life today. But I was just so grateful to be reading about something that was tackling an issue that I couldn't quite put into words myself.

P: I just couldn't get past that certainty he has in having found an answer and badging it up, because I don't believe that life has one, really.

O: There aren't any answers?

P: I re-read *Dancer from the Dance* since we last met. It was given to me by a massively inappropriate boyfriend I had at nineteen. Looking back on it now, and all the very hard lessons it contains in such

8. THE VELVET RAGE

In this 2005 book, psychologist Alan Downs posits that 'velvet rage' is the deeply-held feeling of shame arising from growing up gay in a straight world, often manifesting in mental health conditions and other, more benign, ways of relating to the world that attempt to compensate for this shame, like conspicuous consumer consumption or having careers in the hairdressing sector. Says Downs: 'Because of our childhoods [gay men] are talented at stepping into something that's a mess and cleaning it up and putting a fabulous facade on it.'

a funny and elegant way, I think that reading that book at that time, when I was living in nightclubs, must've almost saved my life by mapping out a future that can go wrong.

O: Oh my God, wow.

P: Is it a happy accident that ...

O: Go on.

P: ... That the words 'years and years' appear in the book?

O: I knew you were going to say that. Sometimes you do feel like there's a cosmic ringing going on in the universe. I'm being sent a message from a different dimension or a different time. It's really powerful, that book. What I remember as well is the amazing depictions of the relationships between gay men and how fraught and chaotic they can be. It really is an amazing book.

P: I always feel like the party in Fire Island at the end of the book must've been Bruce Weber's inspiration for Pet Shop Boys' 'Being Boring' video.

O: Oh, I've never seen that video.

P: You must. Do you see them as predecessors to what Years & Years are doing?

O: I think there's a whole great pantheon of artists and that success is such a weird thing that you have to rely on all the other voices that came before you, you know? You can't have one without the other, and Pet Shop Boys would definitely apply as far as that's concerned. I don't see us occupying the same space, because they are just such a legendary act. They've done so many albums, there are so many brilliant songs; it wouldn't feel right to say there was any other connection though.

P: Did your mum listen to them?

O: No she didn't, actually. I spent some time hanging out with Neil and Chris, you know. It was so amazing to spend time with people who have been around and seen so many things. Going back to *Dancer from the Dance*, something it hits hard is how difficult it can be to maintain friendships with other gay men. You can't take the sex out of it, the emotional baggage, and sometimes it can feel like we're always trying to hurt each other. But then I've found that spending time with people like Neil and Chris, who I think of as legendary idols, and who are at a different stage in their lives, just sharing all that time with each other, I found really powerful and I'm really happy we did it. It's really hard to find that.

9. BORING °

There is a Pet Shop Boys tribute band called Pet Shop Boys Tribute Band.

MUCH APPRECIATED

The very best books that Olly's been given. Thank you!

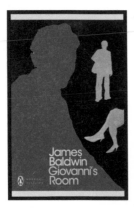 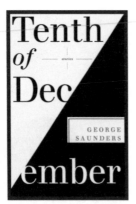  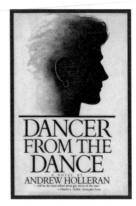

GIOVANNI'S ROOM	TENTH OF DECEMBER	THE VEGETARIAN	DANCER FROM THE DANCE

GIOVANNI'S ROOM
James Baldwin
(1956)

Given to Olly by 'my first boyfriend'

—

The great black American intellectual James Baldwin fled America for Paris in the 1950s, a place where a young homosexual could live and love with relative freedom, away from McCarthy's America, where the 'Lavender Scare' — the witch-hunting of gay men and women — was then in full swing. In *Giovanni's Room*, our narrator — also an American in Paris — falls deeply in love with the intense, troubled Italian bartender Giovanni, and the consequences will haunt him for a lifetime.

TENTH OF DECEMBER
George Saunders
(2013)

Given to Olly by 'my first *proper* boyfriend'

—

George Saunders has become known for surreal, absurdist (yet highly readable) stories, set in an America that we only half recognise, invoking a dreamlike uncanny-valley effect in the reader. In this Folio Prize-winning collection we meet ordinary Americans making their way through life in ways that are slowly revealed to have great cruelty, darkness and shame creeping through the metaphoric white picket fence.

THE VEGETARIAN
Han Kang
(2007)

Given to Olly by 'Holly (one of my oldest and closest friends)'

—

'Before my wife turned vegetarian, I'd always thought of her as completely unremarkable in every way,' begins the first narrator of this bewitching book from the South Korean novelist Han Kang, as he explains how his wife has suddenly, inexplicably, turned vegetarian after a mysterious dream — vegetarianism being a controversial undertaking in South Korea. Various members of *The Vegetarian*'s family take turns to implode as she twists further and further towards the plant-world.

DANCER FROM THE DANCE
Andrew Holleran
(1978)

Given to Olly by 'another boyfriend (we used to joke about getting married)'

—

Fire Island in the 1970s has entered into myth as the gay Mecca; a drive and a ferry ride away from Manhattan, throngs of gay men gathered on its beaches each summer to dance and be free. This book, too, has reached a similar legendary status — it is often called The Gay Gatsby for its portrayal of the beauty and the pain of these hot nights on the dancefloors of Fire Island and Manhattan.

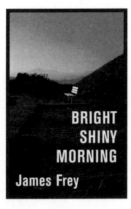

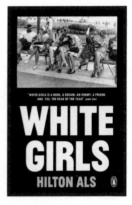

THE EDIBLE
WOMAN
Margaret Atwood
(1969)

*Given to Olly by 'my mother.
I found it on her bookshelf
when I was a teenager'*

—

The first book by the
now-canonical author of
The Handmaid's Tale and
Alias Grace, this novel
follows a young newly-wed
woman who resigns from
her job in market research
after her wedding and then
suddenly starts to see food
as horrifically alive on her
plate — egg yolks are, for
her, yellow eyes staring up,
and she feels the pain of
carrots acutely. If you read
this book after *The Vegetarian*, Margaret Atwood
becomes a spiritual fore-
mother of Han Kang.

BRIGHT SHINY
MORNING
James Frey
(2008)

*Given to Olly by 'a guy
I had a bad one-night
stand with'*

—

A polyphonic portrait of
Los Angeles through a
smattering of characters
living life on its edges:
a narcissistic movie
star, a runaway teenage
couple, ex-beauty queens
and wretched former
child actors. Smattered
with urban legends and
rumours about the dark
history of LA, Frey's novel
cautions us from the very
first line: 'Nothing in this
book should be considered
accurate or reliable.'

THE SEA,
THE SEA
Iris Murdoch
(1978)

*Given to Olly by 'my
literary sister Cara'*

—

Charles Arrowby, play-
wright, director, toast of
the London theatrical
world and an entirely
pompous and self-sat-
isfied man, takes an
isolated house on the
edge of the North Sea in
order to write his Very
Important Memoirs. He
is, improbably, interrupted
by a succession of former
loves, often smashing
things up in the process:
a vase, a mirror, a car.
Notes Charles: 'Human
arrangements are nothing
but loose ends and hazy
reckoning, whatever art
may otherwise pretend in
order to console us.'

WHITE
GIRLS
Hilton Als
(2013)

*Given to Olly by 'a friend
and wise mentor (of sorts)'*

—

Hilton Als — *New Yorker*
theatre critic, Pulitzer
Prize winner and one
of the internet's most
interesting Instagrammers
— explores race, class and
sexuality in prose that
Olly describes as 'loopy...
shifting all the time'.

P: Are there any other gay people in your family?

O: No, and gayness wasn't really spoken about in it. We're a very small family.

P: How did you end up hanging out with Pet Shop Boys?

O: We wrote a song together. It was meant to be a Years & Years song, but we never ended up getting to a place where it worked. I'd love for something to happen with it.

P: Is it a duet?

O: Neil didn't want to sing. But I got him to do some backing vocals on the demo. I think he'd be great singing it.

P: Is fame what you wanted it to be?

O: Definitely not, is the short answer.

P: Why are you laughing when you say that?

O: It feels so embarrassing talking about fame when it's something that you are supposedly a part of, and also if I admit that I wanted to be famous, well, actually that's a bit shameful maybe? I've found myself in this position where there is really a lot to unpack in that question. Fame is also great, in lots of ways.

P: What's the best thing about it?

O: What *is* the best thing about it? I would say that, for me, it's given me more confidence to use my voice. Having millions of people buy your album is quite a good confidence boost, you know? I used to walk into a room and I would feel like the lowest status, littlest piece of shit. That's always how I thought about myself, and now I don't feel that way about myself. I don't feel like I'm better than people. I just feel like it's OK to be me, which sounds ridiculous but it's true.

P: One of the things I loved about the Hilton Als book connects to the feeling that as a gay person you can almost learn by accident to apologise for your presence, by either under- or over-playing it.

O: That's totally true.

P: Either way can feel quite considered. In *White Girls* there is just this ferocious lack of apology for having his voice heard. I found the writing breathtaking in its fearlessness.

O: So many people don't feel comfortable in these spaces — 'spaces', ugh — in the changing room, the pub, the playing field, the classroom, all places that you're expected to be something in. I so knew I wasn't that person and it made me feel so uncomfortable all of the time. Now I don't feel like that. But there are still parts of me that go through those thoughts in my mind. What I was going to say about the Hilton Als book was that I loved the chapters where he was writing about other writers, about Flannery O'Connor and Truman Capote. I didn't actually like *In Cold Blood* that much and his portrait of Capote blew my mind. I was really fascinated by what his opinion was. The things he says about race and sexuality and identity was like ringing a crystal bell and just cutting to this truth, how great it was to be hearing his voice and his experience. It had this really loopy shift back and forth to the personal and fictional. The writing is shifting all the time. What world am I in now? As a writer, he's always making the ground beneath your feet move.

P: That's an excellent description. I'd put that on the book jacket if I was his publisher. There's an amazing observation in the first chapter, which is so simple but so effective, that 'the public only has space for the obvious'. Do you have to be obvious for mainstream success?

O: There's a really good Bob Dylan quote. He says, 'Somebody had to be Bob Dylan and I was the best person for the job.' Something like that, anyway. I've always thought it was such an amazing quote, whatever you think about Bob Dylan. I get this feeling that once you're on the success train, as it were, then everyone else on that train is the public and they are the creators of your success. What they want and what they see is really what you are and you can't stop that train any more. In that respect, if you try and divert too much from it once you've set out your course, you think you might fall off. That's how fame or success or notoriety or whatever just upends your personal perspective.

P: Who'd you want to play the romantic lead in the biopic of your life?

O: River Phoenix. I just fell in love with River Phoenix in *My Own Private Idaho*. I could not believe that film. It had such an impact on me. He's in love with a straight guy and I was in love with my straight best friend and I honestly think, watching that movie, that his performance is art. One of my acting things was always, is it really an art form? Such a terrible thing to say, because obviously it is, but watching River Phoenix in that film made me believe it. I was transported by this man, by his essence, his soul.

P: Have you ever had the feeling that you are playing the part of Olly Alexander in a fictitious story of your own life?

O: Totally. But also, what I've noticed is how many projections there are of who that is. When I meet someone and they know who I am,

---

10. FLANNERY O'CONNOR

Each year on 25 March, which was the American author's birthday, Flannery O'Connor's hometown of Savannah, Georgia stages a parade and street fair in honour of her life.

11. BOB DYLAN

After winning 2016's Nobel Prize in Literature, Bob Dylan delivered a Nobel Lecture in which he focused in particular on the following three books, citing each as a personal inspiration:

– *Moby Dick* by Herman Melville
– *The Odyssey* by Homer
– *All Quiet on the Western Front* by Erich Maria Remarque

(The speech itself was then published as a book although only 100 copies were printed costing $2,500 (£1,882) each.)

they might be projecting something of what they want me to be onto me, and part of that projection is of themselves. We're all just constantly projecting back and forth our hopes for ourselves and for one another. Sometimes I'm like, well, I may as well just play that part of Olly Alexander today because, one, it's my job and I have to do it, and, two, it's really fun and I get to do things that I really love. Number three, and this is where it gets really satisfying, is that it seems to really mean something to people when I play that role.

P: But who is that person?

O: Exactly. You think, well, this person when I'm performing myself — and there is a lot of me in that performance but it's also separate — what am I leaving out of him and what am I taking with me? Some artists get this giant fissure in between them and they cannot separate their public and personal personas. You do have to protect yourself. If you give everything out then there's nothing left. We all know this is a vampiric business. I don't know, obviously, but I think I'm going to be fine because I've had so much therapy about it.

P: You're laughing again.

O: I know. But you see some artists start to become parodies of themselves because they think they know what people want from them. I don't think you ever can.

PAUL FLYNN has worked prolifically as a journalist since the mid 1990s for titles wide across the publishing spectrum. He is the author of *Good As You* (Ebury Press, 2017), a pop-cultural road map to British gay equality, and was part of a small team of co-authors for *Enquirer* (National Theatre of Scotland, 2012), an immersive play concerning the plight of the British newspaper industry. He is the Senior Contributing Editor at *Love* magazine.

THE HAPPY
READER

Love, violence and the allure of the implausible: part two of The Happy Reader is enthralled by Alexandre Dumas' last great pageturner THE BLACK TULIP.

"On 20 August 1672, the city of the Hague, so lively, so white and so trim that you would think every day was Sunday; the city of the Hague with its shady park, its great trees rising above the Gothic houses and the broad mirrors of its canals reflecting the church towers with their almost Oriental cupolas; the city of the Hague, capital of the seven United Provinces, was packed with a red and black stream of citizens in every one of its streets, hurrying, panting, anxious, running along with knives at their belts, muskets on their shoulders or sticks in their hands towards the Buitenhof, that fearsome prison whose barred windows can still be seen today, where Cornelius de Witt, brother of the former Grand Pensionary of Holland, had been languishing ever since the accusation of murder was brought against him by the barber Tyckelaer."

OPENING LINE
A momentous opening sentence. Dumas summons an atmosphere, lowers a political backdrop, names an exact date and location, introduces a major hero, namechecks a minor villain, all while urging the minds' eye to slowly zoom in on a gathering furore in The Hague.

The Book of the Season for this summer, writes SEB EMINA, is a pleasingly florid adventure. A darkness of hue and a surfeit of gore sustain the underrated appeal of Alexandre Dumas' *The Black Tulip*.

FLORICULTURAL THRILLER

A man is trying to grow a flower. There are two reasons why this is difficult. Firstly, he's in prison. Secondly, the flower is one that nobody has ever grown (or seen) before: a tulip that's perfectly black. Handily, he and the jailer's daughter have fallen in love and she's agreed to help him on the condition he loves her more than he does tulips. This is all happening in Holland, by the way. It's the 1670s. Our hero is called Cornelius van Baerle; our heroine goes by Rosa Gryphus. If they can successfully nurture a black tulip they'll receive a sizeable cash prize from the Haarlem Tulip Society.

The Black Tulip is sometimes described as Alexandre Dumas' last great novel. This should probably come with the caveat that the French writer became a household name — one of a handful of writers who are also a station on the Paris Mètro — mostly thanks to his historical blockbusters *The Three Musketeers* and *The Count of Monte Cristo*, books almost everyone has heard of. That this isn't true of *The Black Tulip* is probably thanks to its first chapter, a knot of references to seventeenth-century Dutch politics that seems to be trying to drain a reader's enthusiasm before they can get a foothold in the story. It helps to read up on governmental terms like *stadhouder* (not quite a monarch and not quite a president but comparable to both) and grand pensionary (the elected leader of the States of Holland) — but still, a book club reports to *The Happy Reader* that the experience 'discouraged one member from even turning another page'. Is it worth persevering? Absolutely. The strange but swashbuckling page-turner that follows the exposition is entertaining and unexpectedly memorable. The book club concurs: 'Those who ventured further loved the pace and adventure.'

We're soon witnessing a gory incident from 1672 in which brothers Johan and Cornelius de Witt, political geniuses who had abolished the position of *stadhouder*, are murdered by an angry mob while trying to flee into exile from a prison in The Hague. In Dumas' telling, the incoming *stadhouder*, William of Orange, secretly orchestrates the hate campaign, arranges for the soldiers protecting the de Witts to stand down, then watches from afar as the brothers are torn apart.

I visited The Hague in January. It was like stepping into the arena of *The Black Tulip*, though with a lot more tourist shops and branches of KFC. On a tour of the Buitenhof prison, I poked around the cell where the real and invented versions of Cornelius de Witt were held. Back then, if you had enough money and were thrown in jail, you could pay for a kind of upgrade: with its dark floorboards, four-poster bed and nice view of the Hofvijver pond, the de Witt cell feels less like a prison than a 4.17-star Airbnb flat (marks off for the in-room latrine). Our guide then led us into the torture chamber where, despite the harshest efforts of his enemies, Cornelius de Witt refused to 'confess'.

PENGUIN CLASSICS

ALEXANDRE DUMAS
The Black Tulip

Across the pond at Haags Historisch Museum, I stood inches from the box in which the tongue of Johan and the finger of Cornelius are habitually kept. Various body parts of the de Witts were on sale around the city following their deaths, with fingers for example going for fifteen Dutch sous. The finger and tongue were acquired by supporters days after the murder. Today they were out on loan to another museum. On top of the box, by way of replacement, sat a pair of white 3D printouts.

If Dumas hadn't been so taken with the brothers he would probably have set the story a few decades earlier, when Holland was infected by the speculation bubble known as tulip mania. Between 1636 and 1637 the price of bulbs rose to absurd levels, driven by each buyer's not-unreasonable assumption that someone else would buy the bulbs for an even more inflated sum. Bulbs ended up changing hands for 6,000 guilders each, twice the yearly salary of a relatively well-off merchant, or twenty-four times that of an average carpenter.

The bubble burst but the Dutch love affair with tulips didn't vanish. Instead it went on to become a delightful cliché. That's what *The Black Tulip* is about: the gooey love, not the wild mania. Many believed that this new flower, which arrived in Western Europe via tulip-loving Turkey, was the best of the best, the floral equivalent of *grand cru* champagne or Volkswagen camper vans. 'Among the animals, humans have domination,' wrote the French horticulturalist Charles de La Chesnée Monstereul, 'among the stars, the sun holds first rank; and among the precious stones the diamond is the most estimable; so it is certain that among flowers the tulip carries the prize.'

Which brings us back to Cornelius van Baerle, a tulip worshipper who's in trouble because the de Witts are his godparents. A spying neighbour has denounced him for receiving an envelope from Cornelius de Witt, and now he's stuck in prison. Which is how Dumas turns the growing of plants into riveting adventure, and the tulip into a symbol for just about anything that involves some kind of impossible striving: the work of the artist, the distraction of the lover, the general allure of the unobtainable.

Although, this being fiction, the unobtainable can always, when it comes to it, be obtained.

PSYCHOLOGY

Nobody's immune to the pull of the crowd: if we agree with an angry horde then we are wired to become part of it. But what next? JANE C. HU investigates the age-old process that turns 'I' into 'we'.

BEWARE OF THE MOB

It was the summer of 1999, and MTV was broadcasting pay-per-view coverage as 200,000 festivalgoers descended upon Griffiss Air Force Base in the middle of New York State, for the thirtieth anniversary of Woodstock. The fierce July sun was only intensified by the hot tarmac, but water was on sale for $4 a bottle, and one of the few free water fountains had been smashed in frustration by attendees, leaving a giant mud pit in its place. Waste festered in overflowing latrines, and a layer of trash covered the asphalt.

By the last night of the festival, everyone was overheated, exhausted, feculent. When

Assemblage from a 1931 movie of *Frankenstein* (which as it happens will be Book of the Season in the next issue of this magazine).

the Red Hot Chili Peppers passed out 'peace candles' during their set and launched into a cover of Jimi Hendrix's 'Fire', the agitated crowd lost all control. The candles became the seeds of thirty-foot-tall bonfires, setting alight merch tents and an audio tower. The angry mob raged on, destroying millions of dollars' worth of property, and even stealing an ATM. It took until 3am for 700 New York State troopers to regain control of the base. There was a human toll, too: over the course of the weekend, more than 10,000 people sought medical attention, and dozens of women reported assault or rape.

Woodstock '99 was relatively benign compared to other famous riots across history: the Nika riots in sixth-century Constantinople that burned half the city and killed tens of thousands; the lynch mob that slaughtered the de Witts in 1672; the Los Angeles riots in 1992 that left dozens dead and $1 billion in property damage.

'Crowds are only powerful for destruction,' wrote French psychologist Gustave Le Bon, one of the first academics to consider crowd psychology. His 1895 treatise *The Crowd: A Study of the Popular Mind* laid out a theory that still remains influential in modern-day psychology: something takes hold of each of us in a crowd, allowing our worst instincts to emerge. 'Isolated, he may be a cultivated individual; in a crowd, he is a barbarian— that is, a creature acting by instinct.'

It took about half a century from the publication of Le Bon's book for researchers to probe his claims more empirically. A trio of American psychologists brought young men into the lab and primed them to talk about their parents; in a group setting, they found, the men's comments blurred together. The more the group's identity gelled, the more hostile their attitudes towards their parents became. To describe the process that happens to us as we're 'submerged in the group', the researchers coined the term *deindividuation*.

In more recent years, researchers have explored the conditions which promote or inhibit deindividuation, and the mechanisms behind it. While Le Bon and others believed individuals lose themselves completely when part of a crowd, contemporary researchers think it's a bit more complicated. Even in a mob, our sense of individuality is still in there, somewhere. But it's overtaken by the values of the crowd we're in.

So if we're in a homogeneous, anonymous crowd, it's easier for the consciousness of the group to override our individual norms, which can breed more aggressive, reckless behaviour. In a 1980 study, people were told they had to deliver electric shocks to a stranger to help raise the stranger's heart rate. One group received strong cues of their individuality: they wore name tags, doled out shocks from a brightly lit room, and were told they'd later meet the folks they were shocking. The other group was afforded anonymity: there were no name tags, no post-study meetings, and they worked in a dimly lit room. The more anonymous group assigned stronger shocks.

THE CAST OF CHARACTERS FROM

THE BLACK TULIP

AS IMAGINED BY NEAL FOX

CORNELIUS VAN BAERLE

ROSA GRYPHUS

CORNELIUS DE WITT

JOHAN DE WITT

GRYPHUS

WILLIAM OF ORANGE

ISAAC BOXTEL

It's no surprise that the internet has emerged as the ultimate space for deindividuation. With few cues as to one's real-life individuality, the potential for complete anonymity, and platforms that enable echo chambers, it's easy to lose yourself in whichever online group you're participating in. We see this on Twitter, where thousands of Taylor Swift 'stans' (die-hard fans) threaten anyone who dares to speak ill of their queen, or on Facebook, where racism and misogyny can and do fester in private groups.

As with 'IRL' (in real life) groups, online communities can provide welcome social support, but it's not hard to see how they can also support the flaming, trolling, doxxing, SWAT-ting (calling in a SWAT team to an individual's house via an anonymous 'tip') and other digital expressions of the angry mob mentality. Such attacks have real-world effects: users of the infamous 4chan bulletin board are thought to be responsible for everything from hacking and leaking celebrity nude photos, to doxxing and harassing an eleven-year-old girl to the point of multiple suicide attempts, to countless bomb threats.

There are ways to get people to snap out of this mentality. Cues encouraging self-awareness — such as seeing your reflection in a mirror, or hearing your own speaking voice — have been shown to decrease deindividuation.

In the end, researchers point out that deindividuation itself isn't the culprit of bad behaviour. Its effects are merely a reflection of group norms; in other words, it's only as bad as the group itself. Crowds can also have positive values; charismatic group leaders can, in theory, push a crowd towards adopting them. Consider the subreddit Random Acts of Pizza, which encourages anonymous members to order pizza for strangers. And it might not even be too late for Woodstock to learn from its mistakes — there are rumblings of a Woodstock 2019 to celebrate the original festival's fiftieth anniversary. If it goes ahead, organisers might consider inviting some more wholesome acts.

JANE C. HU is a journalist who writes about the intersection of science and society. She lives in Seattle, but is writing from Longyearbyen, Norway, where polar bears outnumber people.

HORTICULTURE How amazing (and lucrative) — to astonish the world by dreaming up a brand new flower. RICHARD BENSON on the vegetative geniuses racing to find the plant world's next bestseller.

BOTANY NOW

One day in the spring of 1997, an inconspicuous, bespectacled English horticulturalist travelled to a plant growers' show in Holland on the assignment of a lifetime.

Paul Hansord, then the managing director of the Thompson & Morgan seed and plant company, had come to the specialist bulb-growers' event to meet some breeders from Kapiteyn, a small family bulb-growing business based on the flat lands north of Alkmaar.

A few weeks earlier, Hans Kapiteijn, a member of the family (the company and family names are spelled differently), had contacted him at Thompson & Morgan's headquarters in Ipswich with a proposition: a new plant, bred by Hans, that had the potential to make the world's gardeners sit up from their planting and stare with goggle-eyed desire.

At the show, held in an exhibition centre in northern Holland, Hansord found the Kapiteijns among the sweet-scented and vari-coloured displays of tulips, daffodils, crocuses and orchids, and they

1. SEVERAL ◦

From a fascinating ex-
change with star botanist
Mark Dimmitt:

What do you think drives
the extreme interest in
plants that some breeders
seem to have?
    Personally, I've always
been drawn to beautiful
things, and for me that
means brilliantly coloured
and usually complex in
design. In addition to
plants, I'm fascinated
by colourful minerals
(especially crystals), ce-
ramic and glass art (e.g.
Chihuly), and tapestries
(e.g. Maximo Laura).
My plant obsessions are
mostly about those with
brilliant flowers, and some
with bizarre forms such as
welwitschia, boojum trees
and staghorn ferns. Drilling down, my favourite
flowers are eye-dazzling
red. I think that in many
cases what drives the
interest is Asperger's
syndrome. One of the
dominant traits of the
condition is a tendency to
become deeply absorbed
in a single interest, to the
near or complete exclusion
of all other pursuits. I've
long suspected that I'm in
this category, and many
of us call ourselves plant
freaks or plant geeks.

Do you feel you inherited
your love for plants
from your family, who
I have read were farmers
and gardeners?
    My family definitely
helped trigger my interest
in horticulture. While
my parents had no such
interest, the pair of great
grandparents I knew were
farmers who grew a wide
variety of foods. Both
of my grandmothers had
huge flower gardens. I
could get lost in them,
which was very pleasing
to my introverted, self-
reflective personality.

What originally drew you
to plant breeding?
    Long ago I realised
that it was possible to
create varieties of plants
that did not occur in
nature – that I could alter
natural species to better
satisfy my aesthetic

revealed to him three wrinkled, papery bulbs, each about the size of a newborn's fist, and pale magenta-coloured like miniature red onions. Not much to look at, perhaps, but for Hansord it was as if he had been shown dragon eggs. For Hans also showed him the plant that these bulbs would — if Hans was right — produce: a black hyacinth, one of the great chimeras of floriculture.

Hans had been working on the project for more than ten years. 'It took him a long time,' says Charles Valin, current Head Plant Breeder at Thompson & Morgan, 'because hyacinths take a particularly long time to cross-breed. Once you've made a successful cross, it can take four or five years to flower.' Starting out with a blue and a white hyacinth, Hans had painstakingly reselected and recrossed for the darkest colour until the spears of small, fragrant campaniform flowers became so dark they passed for black in all but the brightest sunlight (in reality this is the case with almost all 'black' flowers: the pigments that colour flowers don't exist in pure black, because, it's assumed, they wouldn't attract pollinating insects). More work would be needed to build up commercial stocks, but Hansord was sold.

He bought the bulbs from Kapiteijn at the show for £100,000. Eight years later Thompson & Morgan's black hyacinth, named 'Midnight Mystique', went on sale after a frenzied launch at that year's Chelsea Flower Show. 'This new plant,' wrote the *Guardian*, 'marks the finding of one of horticulture's remaining holy grails, out-romanced in most grower's minds only by the elusive blue rose.' Retailing at £7.99 per bulb (a portion of which goes in royalties to the Kapiteijns) rather than the hyacinth-standard 50p, the 25,000 stock sold out in weeks.

'Midnight Mystique' continues to sell today, though with a relatively small annual supply of between 50,000 and 100,000 bulbs it remains pleasingly rare. It's also a reminder that the obsessions and extrava-gances of seventeenth-century Dutch tulipophiles have their counter-parts in present-day floriculture.

True, prices are unlikely ever to reach those of the tulip mania period, but they still send one's jaw dropping to the mulchy topsoil; in the most lucrative bulb market, galanthophiles (snowdrop fanciers to you and me) have been known to pay more than £1,000 for a single rare specimen. Meanwhile, the world's most expensive plants — rare orchids — fetch upwards of £150,000 at auction.

The pursuit of chimerical plants is pretty common. In the most extreme instance, Japan's Suntory food and drink corporation pro-duces what it calls a blue rose (it is, sad to say, much more lilac than blue). This ongoing genetic modification programme began in 2003 when its flower-loving chairman Nobutada Saji approved the acquisi-tion of an Australian biotech company called Florigene, then known to be working on the rose; the story is given a Dumas-like twist by the rumour that the real motivation, rather than any commercial impetus, was billionaire Saji's own desire to be the first to own this floricultural version of a unicorn.

More prosaically, thousands of breeders around the world are constantly competing to fill niches in the market. Much work is ex-pended on the yellow sweet pea, for example, and on the quest for the perfect, compact, fragrant, flowering evergreen shrub. Black plants remain perennially popular, though no one agrees why. Horticultural writer Karen Platt, author of the definitive book on the subject, *Black Magic* and *Purple Passion*, thinks it's partly because they 'seem to defy nature', and adds that some people are 'horrified' by them. The British plant breeders' agent and astute commentator Graham Spencer says that in the future, breeding quests will increasingly be concerned with plants that can withstand the effects of global warming and associated new diseases.

Competition to hit these niches and secure lucrative sales in garden centres means that new projects in greenhouses and nurseries are carefully hidden and, as in *The Black Tulip*, there is spying and outright theft, or 'midnight breeding'. In 2014, the rare small water lily Nymphaea thermarum was stolen from Kew Gardens; Kew were reluctant to talk about this, but it's not unlikely there was a commercial motivation to the theft, lilies being among the world's most popular plants.

Hitting trends is difficult, though, because as a rule tastes change faster than new plants take to breed, so one might ask what really motivates plant breeders? Charles Valin says breeders 'have varied personalities like everyone else, but they do tend to be very patient and very observant people. You have to have the vision of what might be popular in ten to fifteen years or more, so you need to be kind of a dreamer.'

To better understand what spurs on the world's obsessive botanists, I contact Mark Dimmitt, former Director of Natural History at the Desert Musuem in Tucson, Arizona, and a man famous around the world for both breeding new plants and finding rare ones. In the last two decades the popularity of several plants, such as the brightly flowering adenium, can be traced back to him. Dimmitt offers several explanations for the zeal with which he pursues horticulture, including an obsession with a very particular aesthetic. 'I've always been drawn to beautiful things, and for me that means brilliantly coloured and usually complex in design,' he says. 'Long ago I realised that it was possible to create varieties of plants that did not occur in nature — that I could alter natural species to better satisfy my aesthetic taste.'

The industry can often be corporate and technological, but dreamers do still abound amid its flowers. Take the example of Dr Roderick Woods, now retired but formerly a world-renowned physiologist at

taste. My first successful enterprise was with the California poppy, whose flowers are bright orange. When I was in college in the 1960s, I encountered a variant with dusky red-orange flowers. I collected and grew seeds from that plant, and after about four generations of selection I had a strain with blood-red flowers. (Regrettably, I lost that population when I went too many years without sowing the seeds. To this day there are no California poppies in the trade that are as red as my creation.) When I became obsessed with the genus Adenium in the early 1970s, I saw golden opportunities to develop better horticultural varieties. My ideal for this plant is one with beautiful sculptural form, plus large red flowers that are produced year round. After forty years of breeding, I'm very close to my goal.

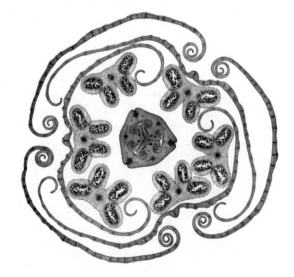

Cross-section of a tulip bud, perceived through a microscope.

IRRIGATION
Tulip fields in Flevoland, east of Amsterdam. Exports from the Netherlands account for 44% of the worldwide trade in floricultural products, putting it far ahead of its nearest competitors Colombia, Germany and Ecuador.

Cambridge University in England. Woods grew up in the English countryside, in a home with a large flower garden, and as a boy he loved hibiscus flowers.

In 1981 Woods was on holiday in the south of France, when his childhood devotion was re-triggered by an unusually bright pink hibiscus plant he spotted in a hedge. Returning to the UK, he began to search for the variety first in nurseries, and then via letter to collectors around the world, but was told it did not exist. Undaunted, he went back to France to find it — only to find it had been obliterated by a road-widening scheme.

Now obsessed, Woods created an image of the original flower using a computer design program and, despite having virtually no experience of plant breeding, set about trying to recreate the variety himself (the original, he concluded, must have been the one-off work of local French bees). Working on his six-acre farm in Norfolk, he made more than 600 crosses, and raised around 10,000 seedlings to flowering age in his quest to find the elusive perfect pink, along the way inventing an entirely new line, the hibiscus 'Chiffon', which is now commonly found in garden centres.

In the early 2000s he at last achieved the pink he had been looking for. 'Pink Chiffon' was released commercially in 2013, some thirty-two years after Woods first glimpsed the flower that inspired it. 'The important thing,' he phlegmatically told writer Tim Woods of new plant blog The Plant Hunter, 'is that the breeder must be obsessed.'

And, one is tempted to add, like anyone who seeks to create something new, perhaps ever so slightly bonkers, too.

RICHARD BENSON is an author and journalist who writes mostly about popular culture. For the last ten years he's had a side interest in recreating a small chalkland wild-flower meadow, which has turned out to be virtually unattainable due to the appetites of selfish rabbits.

MEMOIR

What is a neighbour? Someone who may notice nothing about us — or everything. In the case of *The Black Tulip*, DEBORAH LEVY is reminded of a 'man downstairs' from a former life.

A STRANGE NEIGHBOUR

Surveillance is a creepy word. It suggests the cold, unblinking eye of various disembodied technologies. At least a human spy has eyes that can open and close and cry. When I was twenty-seven I lived on the upper floor of a house divided into two flats. The neighbour who lived on the lower floor was called Mr John. We shared a main front door and a tiny communal hallway to get to our respective flats. I did not know if John was his surname or his first name, and anyway, the mail addressed to his flat was inscribed with a different name all together.

Mr John was already something of a mystery because his eyes were always hidden behind John Lennon-style purple tinted spectacles. He was about fifty and had a shocking abundance of shoulder-length bone-white hair. It was as if the hormones that promote hair growth had accelerated rather than declined in his middle years. He told me he was a philosopher.

Van Baerle doesn't notice the spy next door. Illustration from a 1902 edition of *The Black Tulip*.

One morning, when we were both sorting out the post that flipped through the letterbox of the main door, I decided to test Mr John on some basic philosophical concepts. The problem was that I did not know any basic philosophical concepts myself. Should I ask him if he thought the world was real? And then I remembered a quote from a book I had recently read and asked him if he agreed with Friedrich Nietzsche's lament, 'I cannot believe in a God who wants to be praised all the time.' Mr John smiled. His lips were wide and thin and slightly purple like the lenses of his spectacles. 'Ah,' he said, 'but it is so encouraging to be praised. Perhaps Nietzsche was envious?' I thought that was a magnificent answer. No doubt about it, Mr John was a philosopher of the first order. The few other occasions we spoke in the hallway, he told me it was important to boil an egg for four and not five minutes and that the teaspoon must be laid on the plate pointing towards the egg and not away from it.

At the time, I had a boyfriend who lived in Rome and who visited me every other weekend. When Matteo rang the bell on a Friday, I would run down the stairs to open the door, only to find that Mr John, unfailingly, always got there first.

It was as if my neighbour knew the exact time 'my Roman friend' would arrive and was as excited as I was to see him. The worst thing was that Matteo was excited to see Mr John, too. They would talk in the cramped hallway about all sorts of things — how to cook an artichoke, religious music, traffic problems in Rome and London — while I lurked on the stairs feeling like a gooseberry. Sometimes when we returned to the flat late at night from seeing a movie, Mr John would be hoovering the tiny patch of carpet in the hallway. On these occasions he wore pyjamas and a pair of lace-less Oxford brogues. My neighbour never hoovered the hallway carpet when Matteo was not there.

Then, one Thursday evening, Mr John invited me into his flat for 'a glass of red and a plate of crackers and cheese'. I was curious because I had never seen the inside of his apartment. The only book in his living room was a copy of the *A-Z* of London. He gestured to me to sit on one of the two armchairs. When he was certain that I was sitting and not standing, he told me to 'please bear with him' (as if he intuited he was unbearable) while he prepared the crackers and cheese.

As soon as he was out of the room, I got up from the armchair and walked over to the shelf above his fireplace to look at the postcards that were displayed there. One in particular had caught my eye. It was a blank white card, inked in black fountain pen with the words 'miss you — miss you — miss you'. I knew it was an imitation of a letter that had been written by Man Ray to Lee Miller when they were having an affair in Paris, so I turned the card over to see who was missing Mr John.

It was clearly not addressed to him.

That night I called Matteo to thank him for his card. He told me that he had been quite hurt that I'd said nothing about it. We decided that my neighbour, with his all too human eyes hidden behind his tinted spectacles, was more of a voyeur than a spy. Yet, Matteo was so tender in the way he talked about Mr John, that I wondered if they might both be in love with each other. I could hear an advertisement for a brand of washing-up liquid on his television in Rome. After a while, Matteo said, 'I feel encouraged by the way he praises my route from Heathrow to your flat in the rush hour.'

DEBORAH LEVY's novels include *Swimming Home* and *Hot Milk*, both shortlisted for the Man Booker Prize. The second instalment of her 'living autobiography', *The Cost of Living*, was published recently and she is currently writing a new fiction featuring a spying neighbour and a currywurst wagon in the snow of a Berlin winter.

ART

It's there at the start of Dumas' novel and now it's there on the side of a tower block: AARON PECK on a grim scene from the Dutch Golden Age that's forever being re-rendered.

MURAL MURDER MYSTERY

On the morning of 23 January 2017, the giant figure of a man over eight storeys tall appeared on the side of an apartment tower in Brussels, along the railroad tracks near Chapel Station. He hangs upside down, disembowelled, flesh splayed open, blood trickling down his corpse, his face completely disfigured. While the image echoes those of Abu Ghraib or the atrocities committed by the Islamic State, it instead is sourced closer to home: from a detail of *The Corpses of the de Witt Brothers* (1672–5), attributed to Jan de Baen, located in the Rijksmuseum in Amsterdam. Brussels is famous for its *fresque murales*, of both legal and illegal kinds, but the gory violence of this one was more than a contrast to the charmingly goofy Hergé-inspired murals of the city centre or even the numerous *fresques à caractère sexuelle* that appear in residential neighbourhoods. (Over the same night, another one also appeared near Porte de Flandre, along the canal, based on a detail from Caravaggio's second *The Sacrifice of Isaac* (1603).) Calls were sounded for its immediate removal.

With contemporary Brussels a so-called centre of Islamic radicalisation in Europe, the graffiti seems, at best, politically ambiguous, appearing before the threat of Isis had yet to begin to diminish, less than a year after the Brussels attacks of 22 March 2016. But that provoked a deceptively simpler question: what happens when an image is removed from the story it illustrates? Perhaps inadvertently, the adaptation of *The Corpses of the de Witt Brothers* on that apartment tower in Brussels became part of a long tradition of reproducing the harrowing deaths of the statesmen.

In 1672, Johan de Witt, the Grand Pensionary of the Republic of the Seven United Netherlands, stepped down amid pressures after

FRISIAN
An example of traditional Frisian dress, photographed in the early 1940s yet still channeling the
Rosa Gryphus of 1672.

Unavoidable mural in Brussels, artist unknown.

2. JAN DE BAEN

Earlier that summer of 1672 the killing of the de Witt brothers was prefigured by another incident. It involving a painting by Jan de Baen celebrating Cornelius de Witt's naval prowess. An angry mob in Dordrecht stormed the town hall and seized the painting, ripping it to shreds before nailing de Witt's painted head to the city gallows.

losing battles to France, England, Cologne and Münster, during what became known in Dutch history as the *rampjaar*, or 'disaster year'. Johan de Witt's royalist opponents supported William of Orange, who soon after became *stadhouder* of the Dutch Republic (and later King of England, Scotland and Ireland). Johan de Witt's brother, Cornelius, a military figure and former mayor of Dordrecht, was falsely accused of treason, tortured, and finally sentenced to exile. On 20 August, Johan de Witt entered The Hague's prison to help prepare his brother for exile, when a mob of Orangist militia appeared. William of Orange claimed to have no knowledge of the plan, and was apparently appalled by what happened next.

The mob dragged the de Witts into the street, where they were shot and killed. Afterwards their bodies were strung upside down. The corpses were gutted, like cattle or pigs. The crowd cut off all extremities — lips, fingers, noses, ears, genitals. Body parts were passed around and sold. A finger cost between fifteen and twenty cents. Their hearts were preserved in formaldehyde. Pubs even displayed body parts, like pickled eggs. The tongue of Johan and a finger of Cornelius, safeguarded by sympathisers, were eventually displayed in the Haags Historisch Museum.

Unsurprisingly the story of the de Witt brothers took on the status of a myth. Republicans made them martyrs; Orangists celebrated their deaths as a victory against traitors. Pamphlets often included etchings of the scene, becoming emblematic of the story, based on two contemporaneous paintings: the aforementioned one attributed to Jan de Baen, and *Nocturnal Scene with the Mutilated Bodies of the de Witt Brothers* (1672), attributed to Willem Paets.

It's no wonder that the operatic death and desecration of the de Witts continued to resonate for centuries, not only within the Netherlands, where, for obvious reasons, it became part of the national narrative, but also, in certain cases, elsewhere. In 1850, Alexandre Dumas reimagined the scene of their murder in the third chapter of *The Black Tulip*. In 2015, Roel Reiné's film *Admiral* staged their deaths (there is even a brief scene where we see the arm of a painter applying a brush to the canvas of *The Corpses*, anachronistically painting the picture at night *en plein air* in front of the bodies). And, in 2016, at The Hague, Folkert de Jong's *Dutch Mechanisms* debuted as part of Stroom den Haag's The Sculpture Gallery in the centre of The Hague. In the city square where the de Witts were murdered, de Jong placed two bronze skeletons, as well as 3D prints of the tongue and finger cast in bronze.

And then last January, the mural in Brussels. In every other case, depictions of the de Witts' corpses are always directly related to the story of their murder — through text in a pamphlet with accompanying etching, through the titles of the paintings, through the content and material of a sculpture, through narrative in a novel or a film. In the Brussels graffiti, there's no text, no title, nothing to anchor the image to the de Witts; there's not even two figures, only one. When Belgian reporters mentioned the source image, instead of probing the history or meaning of the source, they debated whether it was an attempt to inspire political violence, or a plea to avoid it. As with most of the illegal *fresques* in Brussels, provocation itself seems to be the goal. In an attempt at ambiguity, the corpse *fresque* fails to shake the story it illustrates. Its history is too heavy. Instead it serves as a reminder that barbarism is a shared condition. As Ezra Pound said, 'Hell is here. Here.'

AARON PECK is a writer and art critic, and author of a novel titled *The Bewilderments of Bernard Willis*. He recently moved from Brussels to Paris, where he runs every morning in the botanical wonderland known simply as the Jardin des Plantes — the Garden of Plants.

Having fallen for his jailer's daughter, Cornelius effectively hopes that the man trying to have him executed will become his father-in-law. That's strange. But as JEAN HANNAH EDELSTEIN shows, marrying into a new family is always pretty risky.

NINE WORST IN-LAWS

LEAH, from the Old Testament, married Jacob, her intended brother-in-law, after her father Laban (himself a bad father-in-law) did a quick bridal switcheroo at the wedding of Leah's sister Rachel to Jacob, putting a veil on the woman who history remembers as the less-hot sister. Afterwards, Laban felt sorry and allowed Jacob to marry Rachel as well. I still wouldn't trust him and I still wouldn't trust Leah.

IXION, a key figure in Greek mythology, pushed his father-in-law Deioneus into a coal fire after he got called out for not paying the full bride price for his wife, which was reprehensible although I, too, find bride price a sexist concept.

HENRY VIII, an English king of the sixteenth century who liked marrying, was a notoriously bad husband, but he was also a bad brother-in-law: after fathering two children with Mary Boleyn, he married her sister Anne Boleyn instead, and was very rude to Mary thereafter. Though some might argue that she won, at the end of the day, by not being executed (she merely died in penury thanks to Henry's lack of generosity).

ELIZABETH ANN DUNCAN, a drifter and one-time madam, was the last woman executed in California, in 1962, and the reason that she was executed was that she arranged the murder of her pregnant daughter-in-law. The murder was a last resort after her other schemes to break up her son and his wife failed. These schemes included pretending to be her daughter-in-law and going to court to have the marriage annulled.

OSWALD MOSLEY, a twentieth-century advocate for fascism in the UK, was the brother-in-law of the journalist Jessica Mitford; she was not a fan. Though Jessica's sister Diana Mosley tried to heal the rift between them, Mitford responded to Diana's invitation for her half-Jewish son Benjamin to spend a holiday with her and his uncle Oswald as follows: 'I thought better not, as I didn't want Benj turned into a lampshade.' Don't you wish you could deliver lines like that to your fascist in-laws next Christmas?

PRINCE PHILIP, the Duke of Edinburgh, the queen's husband, isn't known for his tact, but through the years he's directed much ire towards his daughter-in-law Sarah Ferguson. For though Fergie has such a companionable relationship with her ex-husband Andrew that they still live together, Philip is rumoured to resent her so much for the long-ago marriage break-up that he has said she 'has no point'. To which one might ask: and what exactly are you for? Perhaps she can drop that one at the next royal wedding.

CHARLES KUSHNER, a real estate huckster, was mad at his sister and her husband for speaking to US federal authorities about his dirty political contributions. But instead of freezing them out at Thanksgiving, he hired a prostitute to seduce his brother-in-law in a room equipped with a video camera. Then he sent the tape to his sister. What a dick move.

No wonder his son went on to be the son-in-law of DONALD J. TRUMP, a very bad man, who needs no introduction.

KATHLEEN REGINA DAVIS, not the best mum, was arrested in Florida in 2017 for trying to run her son-in-law over with a car — bad — after he told his wife, her daughter, that he and Kathleen were having an affair. Worse? Apparently Davis was mad at him for ruining her relationship with her daughter by telling her the truth about what was going on.

JEAN HANNAH EDELSTEIN's father-in-law is a very nice man. She lives in Brooklyn, and you can read her memoir, *This Really Isn't About You*, in August.

TRAVEL

The impossibly prolific Dumas wrote around 650 books in just about every genre, including novels, histories, travelogues, true crime and cookbooks. CHARLIE CONNELLY recommends the travelogues.

DUMAS ON TOUR

Spare a thought for the keeper of the Hotel de la Poste in Martigny, Switzerland, during the middle years of the nineteenth century when he was forced to tolerate a stream of French people arriving at his restaurant demanding bear steaks.

He didn't serve bear. He'd never served bear. Bear steaks were not even, as far as he knew, a thing. Yet with galling regularity French travellers would walk in, sit down, wave away the menu, slap the table and demand his finest, most succulent bear.

Some would become quite indignant when informed that while his kitchen was stocked with any number of delicious steaks they were strictly bovine, not ursine.

The slow disappearance of bears from the French countryside was nothing to do with them being eaten.

'But you served one to Monsieur Dumas,' they would insist.

At first the innkeeper had no idea who this Dumas might be until one day a disappointed diner pulled out a book, leafed through the pages, laid it down open on the table and tapped a forefinger on the relevant passage.

The book was *Impressions de Voyage: En Suisse* by Alexandre Dumas, in which the author recounted how he had visited the Hotel de la Poste in Martigny, taken his seat for dinner and been offered bear steak by the innkeeper.

'Once you've tasted it you'll never want to eat anything else,' he recalled being told.

Sure enough the bear steak was delicious and while Dumas ate it his host pulled up a chair and related the story of how the previous week a local man had noticed the pears disappearing from his orchard at night, how he'd hidden with a gun to catch the scrumper, how a 300-pound bear had shown up and started shaking the fruit from the trees, how the man had fired at the bear, how the bear had attacked the man, how a neighbour had been roused by the screams and how, by the time the neighbour shot the animal dead, it had killed the man — and eaten most of him.

'The piece of meat dropped from my mouth as if impelled by a spring,' wrote Dumas.

It was a great story, the perfect anecdote for a travel narrative: a recondite tale, well told, with a punchline worthy of the extended set-up. The trouble was, only half of it was true. The innkeeper had indeed told Dumas the story of the bear that killed the man who owned the pear trees but he certainly wasn't serving up chunks of the animal for dinner. That part was pure authorial invention.

Many don't realise that
Dumas wrote a Robin
Hood novel (*Prince des
Voleurs*) or that this was
the basis for 1991's Kevin
Costner movie *Robin
Hood: Prince of Thieves*

Published in 1837, the travel narrative *En Suisse* was, unfortunately
for the exasperated innkeeper of Martigny, Dumas' first bestseller. It
remained his most successful title until the publication of *The Count
of Monte Cristo* nearly a decade later and led to a clutch of other travel
books, most of which have been all but lost among the sheer volume of
Dumasian production (nearly forty million words published under his
name during his lifetime). Some bibliographies don't even mention
his travelogues, which is a great pity as his travel writing, showcasing
his immense literary gifts, eye for a good story, natural curiosity and
fizzing, ego-fuelled charisma, offers an enlightening insight into the
man and his extraordinary life.

The best travel writers treat the reader as a companion, guiding and
informing, sharing the highlights and disasters of their journey to forge
a footsore intimacy with the person reading the book. In Alexandre
Dumas' travelogues he grasps the reader by the coat sleeve and drags
them with him, battering through deserts and across seas at a frequent-
ly bewildering pace, all the while pointing, lecturing and hectoring
in exhaustive detail (the four-volume *De Paris à Cadiz* was based on
a journey of just eight weeks). As his fame grew and he progressed up
the social ladder, the reader could find themselves left outside while
Dumas disappeared to dine with counts and princesses; indeed the
itinerary of his 1860 journey through Tsarist Russia from Finland
to the Caspian Sea, published as *En Russie: De Paris à Astrakan*, was
partly defined by estates belonging to an aristocratic Russian family
he'd befriended on the Paris party scene. Yet for all his social climb-
ing Dumas seemed as happy to lay his head on the stained and lumpy
pillows of commercial travellers' inns as the luxury goose down of
country estates, and as a travel writer he was never anything less than
addictively irrepressible company.

Dumas never felt he received the credit he deserved at home, so
it's perhaps no wonder he was so keen to travel whenever the oppor-
tunity arose. 'Posterity begins abroad' was one of his favourite say-
ings, something he learned in 1846 when, at the height of his fame, he
embarked on a journey through Spain to North Africa. France had just
taken colonial possession of Algeria and was keen to encourage French
settlers to relocate. What better way to promote the region than a book
by the nation's most famous writer? The Ministry of Education placed
an entire warship, *Le Véloce*, at his disposal to cross the Mediterranean
and asked only that he call in at Madrid on his way south to attend the
wedding of the Infanta on the government's behalf.

Dumas was uncharacteristically nervous when he approached the
Spanish border. A keen huntsman, he had in his luggage what amount-
ed to a small arsenal, designed to dispatch a wide range of animals
on his travels, despite the non-tolerance of the Spanish regarding the
transport of arms across their territory. When Dumas reached the cus-
toms post, however, as soon as officials read the name on the luggage
labels he was escorted across the border with obsequious regard by
the men, who wouldn't have dreamed of examining the baggage of the
eminent Dumas.

'As you cross the frontier, it is as though you pass from this life to
the next,' he wrote in *De Paris à Cadiz*. 'It is not to you but to your
shade that all these testimonies of affection at every turn of the road
are addressed; and I must say that my glorious shade is received in this

DOMINANT SEAT
The House of Orange sat here. They have sat on a lot of thrones. *The Black Tulip* opens at that moment when William of Orange craftily cements his grip on power. He succeeds so thoroughly that over three hundred years later the Dutch royal family are still drawn from his dynasty.

SUBMISSIVE SEAT
Bondage chair of a kind once found in the rooms of the Black Tulip Hotel, Amsterdam: 'Europe's finest art and leather hotel.' The hotel, which closed in 2010, offered in-room BDSM facilities as well as minibars, TVs, etc.

country with such acclaim as to make my poor mortal soul quite envious. From the flattering picture the Spanish form of me I have some inkling of what people will think about me after my death.'

The Spanish and North African adventure of the mid 1840s that produced both *De Paris à Cadiz* and *Le Véloce, ou Tanger, Alger et Tunis* was arranged at short notice and kept him away from France for a whole year, much to the litigious displeasure of several newspapers and periodicals who were part-way through popular — and expensive — serialised Dumas stories when he packed his steamer trunk, snatched up his cane and bustled south.

Travelling gave Dumas respite from a tumultuous personal life — one biographer has identified forty mistresses — and the sniping at home of contemporaries who resented his domination of both the book and magazine serial markets, so such nourishment of his colossal ego as he received at the Spanish border was always welcome and became a feature of his travels. During the journey he made for *En Russie* he endured a long, rough steamer voyage during a terrible storm to visit a remote island monastery where he found the abbot delighted to meet him as he knew all about *The Three Musketeers* and *The Count of Monte Cristo*. In remote Saratov he stepped ashore from his voyage along the Volga to see a lingerie shop run by a Frenchwoman who knew who he was as soon as he walked through the door. Later the Kazan chief of police deliberately manufactured a problem with a ship's paperwork in order to delay it long enough for Dumas to go hunting for a day before continuing his Volga journey.

'Despotism may have its drawbacks,' wrote the noted republican, 'but on occasion it can be a great convenience.'

For all his prolificacy — one newspaper cartoon published at the height of his career showed Dumas having soup poured into his mouth while he scribbled away with two pens in each hand — the travel narratives are probably as close as we come to knowing the real Alexandre Dumas through his writing. There is exaggeration in the stories, but for all the hard beds and terrible food — a constant complaint from a man who compiled a *Grand Dictionnaire de Cuisine* — it was on the road that Dumas appeared happiest, whether lampooning the British at Gibraltar ('There was no fog at Gibraltar until Gibraltar was annexed by the British. The British were used to fog, didn't feel at home unless there was fog, so they made fog') or treating the *Véloce* as a charter yacht rather than a ship of the line and awarding himself a 21-gun salute while sailing into Tunis harbour ('Tunis, courteous as always, returned our salute, perhaps not as promptly or correctly as we would have wished').

'To travel is to live in the full meaning of the word,' Dumas wrote. 'The past and the future are swallowed in the present; one fills one's lungs, takes pleasure in everything and holds all of creation in the hollow of one's hand.'

Just don't ask for the bear steak.

CHARLIE CONNELLY is a travel author. His books include the bestselling *Attention All Shipping: A Journey Round The Shipping Forecast*. He is the literary correspondent for *The New European* and has never tried bear steak.

The story of Cornelius testifies to the handiness of homing pigeons, but what of the pigeon today? As THOMAS BIRD here reports, the centre of the pigeon-fancying world is no longer the Netherlands or Belgium but China, and the sums of money involved are enormous.

THE GOLDEN PIGEON

Miyun is a Beijing satellite forty miles northeast of the capital as the crow flies. The town is located at the junction of the North China Plain and the Yanshan Mountains, and parts of the Great Wall can be distinguished crowning the nearby hills, making it popular with weekenders. Much of the old architecture has been lost to modernity, although a few low-rise traditional houses survive. It's in this old quarter that I meet train driver Zhang Jiantao who, when he's not puffing through the People's Republic, cares for his pigeons.

'I started keeping pigeons in the 1980s, not long after I started driving trains,' says Zhang, who is something of a trailblazer when it comes to pigeon fancying.

Keeping domestic birds has been popular in China since the Qing dynasty. Even today a brief wander through Beijing's *hutongs* (old alleyways) will offer glimpses of locals walking their caged warblers. But cast your attention to the rooftops and it won't be long before you catch the cooing of pigeons.

According to recent estimates, China is home to over 300,000 fanciers while the pigeon strongholds of Europe, namely Holland and Belgium, have seen a stark decline: in the 1950s the Belgian Royal Pigeon Association boasted 250,000 members; these days it barely touches 30,000.

China not only belies the trend in popularity, it is also inflating pigeon prices to premiership football levels. So-called 'princelings', Beijing's nouveau riche, have garnered notoriety for splashing out on luxury goods, from French wine to contemporary art. President

A fast and reliable form of communication.

Xi Jinping's war on corruption has provoked a more subtle spending culture among these elites. But still, the billionaires appear to have found a new foreign fetish to give the star treatment to. Curiously, it's the humble pigeon.

Recent headline grabbers include Xing Wei, a property tycoon, who paid almost £350,000 for a Belgian pigeon in what was reported to be the largest deal on record. Chinese interest has pushed the value of thoroughbred birds up threefold in a decade. While this is fantastic news for Belgian and Dutch master-breeders, it does raise the question: why are the Chinese going cuckoo for pigeons?

Europeans first introduced homing pigeons to China, but after the revolution of 1949, Chairman Mao had them banned, except for military communications. When China cautiously reopened its doors after the catastrophic Cultural Revolution, a flock of foreign ideas made landfall, including pigeon fancying.

Like many Chinese men, Zhang is quite fanatical about his pastime; he has pigeon posters on the walls and exhibits his trophies proudly. The eldest of his 100-strong flock is a startling eighteen years old, while the juniors pecked through their eggshells just a few days before my visit. It's a veritable community, as intimate as a traditional Chinese village, with each one unique to its owner in appearance or temperament.

His patience and passion is representative of how most Chinese pigeon fanciers have nurtured their brood since the reform era, but the boom economy has brought pigeon fancying to a much wider (and richer) audience. Centred on exclusive clubs like the Pioneer Loft in Beijing, pigeon racing has turned fancying into a fruitful endeavour; the prize pot for their annual 500km 'Iron Eagle' race series was north of £50 million this year.

When Zhang is asked about the murky world of gambling that has arisen in concert with pigeon racing he says, 'Nobody's really monitoring it. If they do it will stop, until then…' He raises his eyebrows, suggesting the future is unclear.

What does seem evident is that while pigeons continue to fly *over* the authority's radar, a new class of fanciers are making a rich man's game of a poor man's pastime, accompanied, of course, by big money's attendant ills.

THOMAS BIRD is a Beijing-based writer from the UK. He likes train travel, craft beer and the teachings of Zhuangzi.

Having been enticed by the promise of her own black tulip, REBECCA MAY JOHNSON records a wonderful winter spent staring at the ground.

QUEEN OF THE NIGHT

OCTOBER — The photograph of deep purple satin-textured flowers on the packet of bulbs at the Dulwich pot and plant centre makes my pupils dilate. The almost black petals were the outcome of Dutch flower breeder J.J. Grullemans's attempt to produce a black tulip in 1944. He called his creation Queen of the Night. It was one of many such attempts during the twentieth century and still none have yet succeeded. Like a truly blue rose, the creation of a black tulip eludes and obsesses the wit of horticulturalists.

When I was a child I was a worshipper of plants. I lived among fields at the end of a long, dead-end road in a Suffolk village and we had no neighbours. I watched the place where snowdrops grew with great devotion. I had never seen my mother plant them (though she must have) and so I felt sure that the snow itself summoned the flowers when it changed the landscape to white. Like the fairy ring of mushrooms that came up nearby at other times of year and the eruption of

TOOLS

1. In the garden, order can only really be maintained by way of targeted anti-weed brutality, as per this ash-handled DeWit Bio Daisy Grubber.
2. A turnip pick, with its built-in gathering blade, is catnip to anyone who likes mono-purpose design.
3. Gardenware brand DeWit, whose name of course recalls *The Black Tulip*'s de Witt brothers, are behind this comby hoe, with a three-tine head for cultivating.
4. This torture hammer can be viewed in the Prison Gate Museum in The Hague. It's the exact same building where Cornelius de Witt was tortured, in the name of something calling itself order.
5. The best way to ensure one's cucumber is perfectly level is by removing its options for deviance, hence these prophylactic-seeming cucumber straighteners.
6. To separate undesirable elements from soil, try an 8-inch Garden Riddle by Objects of Use.
7. These Spear and Jackson Single-handed Grass

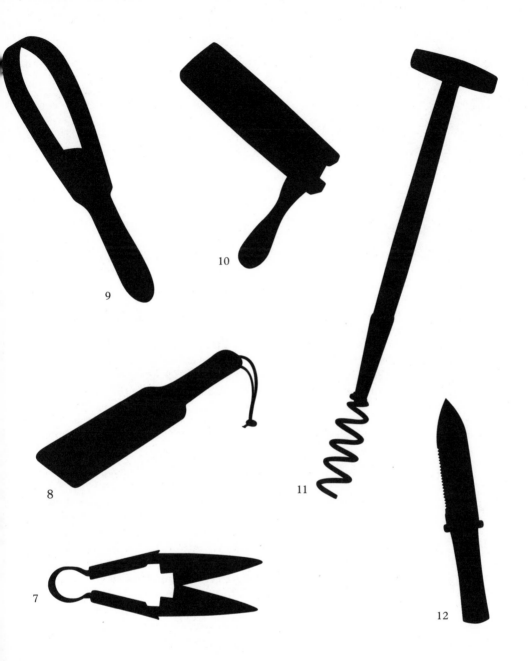

Shears are ideal if kneeling on the turf border, wishing to bring the lawn's edges to an enviable neatness.
8. This isn't a garden tool at all but a bondage paddle.
9. The nunki weeder's comfortable beech handle and sharp curved blade allow gardeners to loosen weed roots and destroy mat-forming weeds with no risk to nearby legitimate plants.
10. Weeds aren't the only obstacle to harmony. Ward off birds, for example, with this bird scarer rattle.

11. They're the toughest plants, so why does 'weedy' mean weak? Drilling with this DeWit Dandelion Weeder will get to the higher parts of the dandelion, but soon enough — it'll be back.
12. At the trial of Cornelius van Baerle, a judge observes that 'it was proved in history that many very dangerous men were engaged in gardening.' A *hori hori*, such as this by DeWit, is also known as a Japanese soil knife.

The first tulip bulbs in Europe were mistaken for a kind of onion, and eaten.

white cow parsley in late May, the arrival of the snowdrops seemed beyond us. Now, when I mention my intention to grow tulips, people pass on scraps of knowledge and I begin to understand the complex biological conditions that produced the flowers I watched as a child. The cashier in the plant centre tells me to place a small handful of gravel under each bulb so that the water will drain from under them and they won't rot in the ground. An acquaintance warns me off planting them before it is truly cold, or they will sprout too soon without flowering. The cold kills off dangerous viruses and bacteria, too. I buy a bag of gravel and wait for temperatures to drop.

DECEMBER — I search for the key to the shed. The garden of every house on our estate has a robust brick shed and all gardens face south, so you can even grow tomatoes uncovered and they will ripen. A man across the way is mad for dahlias and in early autumn they put on a razzle-dazzle show of brilliant colour. I look our development up and discover that we live on 'The Dutch Estate', designed in 1965 and named because of a twinning arrangement between Camberwell and Deventer in the Netherlands. Dutch civic dignitaries visited up until the 1980s. Every 'way' is called after a Dutch artist or town; mine is named after the fourteenth-century religious scholar Thomas à Kempis, who gave his books the names of flowers. I am flabbergasted by all this. My decision to grow tulips feels right.

I unlock the door and inhale the smell of northern European shed-damp. I look through bicycles, white plastic furniture and bamboo poles to find the hand fork and the end of a bag of compost. I turn to my task. I grub up mounds of soil and make little holes, drop in a small handful of gravel as instructed, then a handful of compost, then the bulb and cover it over with the displaced earth. I feel myself becoming careless as I go, as I do when I perform any repetitive task. I dot the bulbs across the two flower beds, filling in any space there's a gap. The earth still hasn't frozen and I am caught between wondering if the mild conditions will ruin the bulbs and the possibility I've left it too late for them to flower next spring.

JANUARY — My friend Dr Christopher Douse, a Future Leader Fellow in biochemical science at Cambridge University, pipes up to mention the required 'chilling time' of twelve to sixteen weeks needed by tulip bulbs to ensure they flower, 'a beautiful example of epigenetics', he says. I am baffled and he explains via email.

I am glad to learn about epigenetics but it makes me more anxious about the success of my tulips. I'm sure they won't spend long enough in this state of critical, freezing gestation, an idea that nonetheless strikes me as wonderfully perverse. I also find out about the importance of depth: various online sources recommend burying the bulbs at least eight inches deep and pointing upwards — mine are only four inches deep. I have no idea which way they are pointing.

FEBRUARY — Reddish-green spear-like shoots have come up through the ground.

They are getting taller quickly, but I notice that some of the leaves have small holes in them. Initially I wonder if it's a slug. When I was planting the bulbs in December a friend told me that hers were consumed by slugs. But on that front I have been vigilant, I think.

MARCH — When I am examining the soil in search of slugs, I disturb some small flea-like beetles that begin hopping around. I find out that my tulips are under attack by 'flea beetles', which have eaten a rash of ugly blemishes into the Queens' matte, eau de Nil leaves. This upsets me. I research feverishly how to get rid of them, wondering if they're fatal. I don't have much luck. Another morning I notice that something has dug up soil around the tulips, damaging one of them. Is a neighbour's cat shitting among my bulbs? Is it the screeching parakeets that roost on a nearby tree? Or the blackbird I feed? Is this what brought the fleas? Harrumph!

APRIL — It was the blackbird.

The month begins on Easter Sunday with torrents of rain and I stare out of the window, begging for sunshine. I think about the Queen of the Night every day. When I walk past the bed where I buried the bulbs I think about their flowers arriving in May and almost see the almost black petals, a contrary resurrection of winter's shade in spring. I think I can see a flower stem coming up through the leaves.

I feel an affinity with Cornelius van Baerle's fixation on his tulips; his attendance to the physical needs of his cultivars and strong emotions when they are threatened. I too have monitored temperature, moisture, and manifold threats to their survival. I have turned my life towards the earth and felt the concerns of the tulips. The grinding blankness of winter has been transformed into a gestation replete with possibility: I have been given succour by waiting for the bloom of flowers I have yet to see. If they never come I will still have had this nourishment.

Today is the first warm, sunny day of the year and I have been delivered safely into spring by the Queen of the Night.

4. EMAIL

'Epigenetics are changes in organisms caused by modification of gene expression rather than alteration of the genetic code itself. In other words, think of the genome/genetic code as a series of musical notes (B flat, C, D) written down on a page. It can be played in multiple different ways. This is vvv important to our survival. All the different cells in our body (or in a tulip plant) carry the same genetic code. But there has to be a way to differentiate between (say) a cell in your eye, and a cell in your heart. We also need ways to adapt to our surroundings.

The organism has several ways that it can control the way the genes are expressed. Importantly, these can be influenced by the environment. In some plants, there is a response to the cold which leads to an attenuation in the expression of a particular gene important in controlling when the plant flowers. As winter progresses, its expression continues to decrease. By the time spring comes, this barrier to flowering has been removed, and you get flowers. I think the process is called vernalisation, or, the cooling during germination in order to accelerate flowering when it is planted. This is an epigenetic phenomenon. All the cells in the plant have this gene but the timing of its expression is critical.'

REBECCA MAY JOHNSON is a writer, academic and budding gardener based in London and working at Newcastle University. She is a keen helmswoman and hopes to sail to the Netherlands before too long. She is writing a book about food and being a woman.

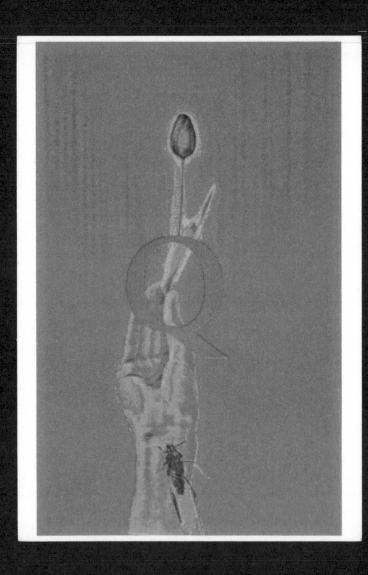

Correspondent ROB
MEERMAN's innovative
postcard from the 1990s
(see letters, right).

LETTERS

Hypnotic stains, one-track brains and design software
of the early '90s.

Dear Seb, hello Happy Reader,

I'm amused to learn of this season's communal read, *The Black Tulip*, as it reminds me of my graduation project of which I'm attaching this postcard (pictured, left). I studied graphic design at Amsterdam's Rietveld Academy and in 1991 my final thesis was an investigation into the black tulip. My medium was a desktop computer, which was a rare and new (and crazily expensive) thing at the time. I can't remember why I chose the *black* tulip as my subject other than the eternal holy grail of making a truly black flower, which perhaps I linked to the mysterious future possibilities of the computer? Did my subject, subconsciously, even predict the dotcom bubble, arguably a sort of Tulip Mania of our times? I made my thesis in a program called SuperCard, the colour successor to HyperCard, and of course nothing of it remains but this paper postcard — how ironic that a paper print outlived my early digital endeavours. What puzzles me, thinking back of my graduation and how I approached my research at the time, is that I never read Dumas' book!

Rob Meerman
Amsterdam

Dear Happy Reader,

Ever since the first issue came out, I've been a very happy reader indeed. However, I had a very tumultuous relationship with the last book of the season. Or, to be more precise, with D-503. Unlikable characters have never bothered me that much, but I just couldn't get over my dislike for this particular specimen. As I see it, *We* is not so much a story about oppressive state power and 'the dangers of developing a soul', but rather about sex as the most terrifying power of all. D-503's internal struggle didn't arise from a sudden realisation that his orderly little world was not so perfect after all, his problem was an insatiable desire for one particular woman. He wanted to do certain things to her, and he wanted to be the only one. In that regard, D-503 certainly didn't long for any kind of personal freedom, quite the opposite — complete control over I-330 would have been preferable so that he could be with her 'each minute, every minute, alone'. We all know how the story ended when that fantasy didn't come to fruition … She got punished.

While Zamyatin's style and ideas were surprisingly modern for the time, in a sense he has written yet another version of the oldest story in the world.

Sincerely,
Paula Avota
Latvia

To The Happy Reader,

I've long dreamed of working in the archives of an atelier or curating fashion and costume, and so I found comfort in Aaron Ayscough's tale about Parfait Elève de Pouyanne ('As Good As New', *THR10*). It struck a cord in my heart. I now find the technicalities of dry-cleaning to be somewhat mesmeric; and I walk past my local cleaners with wide eyes, often wondering of the stories behind the stains.

I hope that my future wedding dress never becomes bloodstained, but if it does, I'm taking my gown to Paris.

Marianne Michael
London

The Happy Reader accepts letters in all available modes including email at letters@thehappyreader.com or snail mail at The Happy Reader, Penguin Books, 80 Strand, London WC2R 0RL.

The Happy Reader is published twice a year, in summer and winter. Receive each issue as soon as it's out by subscribing at thehappyreader.com.

NOW READ FRANKENSTEIN

It's summer now but the snug nights of winter are looming. The next issue of *The Happy Reader* is also in the works. In winter 2018, the Book of the Season is a horror story that has resonated through the centuries. It's *Frankenstein*, a Gothic tale written exactly two hundred years ago, in 1818, when its author, Mary Shelley, was just eighteen years old.

The basics of the story are well known. Man plunders graveyard. Man creates monster. Understandably unhappy monster decides to destroy man. Yet as with many of these ubiquitous classics, the broad brushstrokes of which we seem to pick up by a kind of cultural osmosis, how many of us have secretly never read the original? And even for those who have, isn't it a book that demands to be re-read and reassessed from time to time?

It seems incredible in hindsight, but the *Frankenstein* of 1818 met with underwhelming reviews. 'It gratuitously harasses the heart,' complained *The Quarterly Review*. Now, of course, it's virtually impossible to go a week without encountering a reference to the book. It's a cast-iron fact that at this exact moment, somebody somewhere is saying, 'The monster wasn't called Frankenstein, you know. Frankenstein was the name of the doctor.' The book's lasting influence is hardly surprising. Driverless cars, artificial intelligence, GM crops, drone-based paparazzi: over the last two hundred years the unintended effects of science have hardly faded into irrelevance.

Have you read *Frankenstein*? What did you think? Please send all letters to be printed in the next issue to letters@thehappyreader.com or Penguin Books, 80 Strand, London WC2R 0RL.

Jacket for *Frankenstein*, originally published in 1818.